Unrefined

Watch for more special collectors edition books in this series.

Unrefined

A Hungry Hollow Tale

Sharon Balts

LIFE SENTENCE
Publishing, LLC

www.lifesentencepublishing.com

Unrefined – Sharon Balts

Scriptures taken from the Holy Bible, King James Version.

Printed in the United States of America

First edition published 2014

LIFE SENTENCE Publishing books are available at discounted prices for ministries and other outreach.
Find out more by contacting us at info@lspbooks.com

LIFE SENTENCE Publishing and its logo are trademarks of

LIFE SENTENCE Publishing, LLC
P.O. Box 652
Abbotsford, WI 54405

Paperback ISBN: 978-1-62245-167-8

Ebook ISBN: 978-1-62245-168-5

10 9 8 7 6 5 4 3 2 1

This book is available from www.amazon.com, Barnes & Noble, and your local Christian bookstore.

Cover Design: Amber Burger

Editor: Emily Davis

Share this book on Facebook:

Contents

[I] will refine them as silver is refined, and try them as gold is tried. (Zech. 13:9, KJV)

Acknowledgements

While creating an historical fiction story that cites a popular farm show and features machinery from by-gone days, I have discovered something wonderful. Tractor club members, farm show buffs, and collectors of North America's farm history are a delight to work with. They have shown much enthusiasm about my latest endeavor and have readily shared their knowledge and experience with me. Many people have had a part in the creation of this story and the other tales that will follow. I appreciate each and every contribution.

My husband Doug is my technical advisor, the one I go to first when I need to know about a piece of machinery or a tractor or an old automobile. Thank you, Doug, for being such a great resource and for being so supportive of this project. I admit, it took me awhile to become an avid farm show buff, but each show we attend offers so much information and such a wonderful look back into history, I now look forward them. I am taking more notes, more pictures, and have a great agenda in putting together this "farm show" collection of novels. I look forward to experiencing more shows with you.

Doni Cripe and I were tending the entrance gate at the Hungry Hollow Steam & Gas Engine Club's show two years ago when she suggested I write a book about the area near Brill, Wisconsin where the club started. She urged me to get it done before the Prairie Gold Rush three-day show in 2014. It took me a while to get a vision for this story, but I finally undertook the project. Thanks, Doni, for being a great fan of my fiction novels and for giving me that wonderful suggestion.

There have been countless conversations from years ago, such as those I have had with my parents and with Doug's parents, that now spark ideas from which I can launch a story. I appreciate that they and many family members shared their remembrances with me.

Member Ann Nelson offered some of the Hungry Hollow club's souvenir booklets as research material. Duane Nelson and other tractor buffs answered questions about Twin City and Minneapolis Moline tractors. As ideas unfolded, there were people like Len Scheiffer, Charlotte Prock, and Bruce Ward who gave me information that sparked further ideas. Thanks to all of you for helping me along the way.

Arvid and Kay Hanson, avid tractor show attendees, were my encouragers. As soon as I spoke to them of doing a collectible series of stories from farm shows around the country, I saw the interest that such a project might generate. Thank you, friends, for your support.

I knew a collectible series of stories was a great idea, but if I was going to get the first book printed in time for the June 2014 show, I was going to have to find a very understanding publisher. Jeremiah Zeiset from Life Sentence Publishing in Abbotsford, WI told me his company could do it. He and the staff have been so helpful to this project. Thank you, Jeremiah, for all you are doing to make this dream a reality.

As soon as I contacted Cheryl DeLap, editor of the Prairie Gold Rush magazine, she promised her help. She asked Prairie Gold Rush member Tony Thompson for pictures of Twin City tractors and one of Tony's tractors graces the cover and interior of this book. Cheryl, your insight helped us perfect the front cover. Your enthusiasm and interest have been a great blessing to me and I appreciate what you have done for this project. Thank you for mentioning my novel to your club members. Thank you, Tony, for sharing your photos.

I look forward to presenting this volume—the Prairie Gold Rush Special Edition—at this year's Hungry Hollow Steam & Gas Engine Show. I appreciate each and every one who shows interest in my stories. I will continue to strive to give readers delightful, wholesome tales and I hope that you, like me, anticipate many more great stories to come.

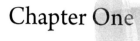

Chapter One

Brill, Wisconsin, late June 1933

Amos shoved at the door of his Model A, which opened in protest. He slid out of the driver's seat, stepped onto the untidy lawn, and solemnly surveyed the tired old farmhouse his daughter Millie called home. Windows that should have been open to the cool morning breeze were closed. The curtains were drawn tight and the place was eerily quiet. Amos felt a stab of alarm.

He moved on trembling legs to the back door – the one he always used when calling on Millie and her husband Ralph. His stomach knotted. When he knocked, Amos' quest for entrance went unanswered, but the knob gave way as he turned it. He backed away in fear. Ralph and Millie had moved to northern Wisconsin from Chicago, where doors had locks and those locks were not left unused. They lived with those same habits here. *Something is wrong! Their car is gone. If Ralph took it to work, Millie would be here. She should have answered my knock...*

With the toe of his worn and dusty boot, Amos cautiously nudged the door. It swung slowly on squeaky hinges, spilling morning light into the dim interior.

"Anybody home?"

A muffled echo answered Amos' booming baritone voice. The thought crossed his mind that he should go for help. *For what?* he reasoned. *You're seventy years old, you old fool. You got no reason to get spooked just because Millie isn't home. She and Ralph probably took the boy for a ride. Maybe they went to the store.*

He moved cautiously inside, studying corners, doorways, walls and tabletops. He was treading as lightly as a burly man could, yet the sound of Amos' steps clapped softly against the walls of the kitchen and parlor as he moved through them.

Millie's standard of housekeeping had always allowed for a good amount of disorder. Today, he found the place to be tidy. Too tidy. And, it was not due to things being put in their proper places. They were missing!

Amos' heart pounded harder as fear tightened its grip. At the bottom of the stairs, he called out once again and got the same distant answer as before. He drew in a deep breath and exhaled loudly. *Stay calm,* he told himself. *Keep your head straight. Think this through.*

Amos had always known his son-in-law had not been the most honest businessman in Chicago. He wondered now if Ralph's past had caught up with him. *Chicago's mob wouldn't bother coming this far north for a two-bit con man like Ralph, unless he knew something... or someone....*

Amos began a second search of the premises, deliberately looking for clues as to his daughter's whereabouts and trembled at the realization that he was looking for blood. He found none. He didn't see any bullet holes or signs of struggle either. To his relief, there was no indication that Millie or Ralph had been attacked or forced to leave. Yet, they seemed to have left in haste, as indicated by the foodstuffs loitering in the room-temperature ice box. Their personal things were gone: clothes from the closets, jewelry, Ralph's shaving mug that always sat on the windowsill...and Joey. Except for a small wooden truck tipped on its side, lying under a chair, nothing indicated that a little boy had been here.

Amos bent slowly and picked up the toy and then sat down

heavily on the chair. He rubbed his calloused hand over the smooth sides of the vehicle and recalled the hours he had spent cutting, gluing, and sanding to fashion it. The look of delight on Joey's face when Amos had presented him with the gift had made every minute of his labors worthwhile. The truck was so precious to the little boy that he carried it everywhere with him. *Why was it left behind?*

Wrenching sobs overtook the old man. "How could Millie do this?" he wailed. "How could she run off with her own sister's child?"

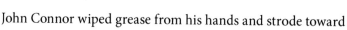

John Connor wiped grease from his hands and strode toward his father-in-law's coupe in anticipation of giving his little boy a giant hug. "I sure miss the little rascal," he said to himself. "We should have brought him home weeks ago."

As he strode toward the vehicle, John's daughter Irma rushed from the house with baby sister Dorothy on her hip. She joined her father as he approached the Model A. There, they found Amos sitting silently in the cab with tears in his eyes and holding Joey's little toy truck in trembling hands.

"Amos? What's wrong? Where's the boy?"

John's heart began pounding like a hammer upon his heavy anvil as he awaited an answer. At first, Amos said nothing, just shook his head and groaned. His shoulders sagged as though under a heavy burden. He finally managed to choke out the words, "They're gone."

"What do you mean, gone?"

"Ralph and Millie... and Joey. They're not there."

John's words were desperate ones as he tried to comfort Amos and convince himself the pangs of fear that were assaulting him were unfounded.

"They've made friends with folks in town. And... and there

are relatives around. They're just off visiting someone. We'll go back to the house tomorrow and get Joey. It'll be all right, Amos."

Amos knotted his bushy gray brows together and looked down at the steering wheel.

"They've been gone for days, John. They took their clothes and personal stuff and left food lying around that's gone bad."

John's face paled. He cast a worried glance at Irma, whose eyes were wide with fear.

"Are you *sure* they took Joey? They didn't leave him with someone? A neighbor? Or... or the pastor?"

Amos shook his gray-haired head. "I asked the neighbors. The Gustafsons saw Ralph and Millie load up the car with suitcases and carry the boy out of the house. Joey waved to them when they went by. They assumed Ralph was taking the boy home, but they did think it was strange that they hadn't seen him and Millie around for a few days."

Amos' voice quivered. He blinked rapidly to dispel his tears. "I looked all around the place before I went to the neighbors. Sad that a man doesn't trust his own daughter, but I was half afraid I'd find a grave. I didn't find one, thank God."

John's voice rose to a desperate pitch. "Where would they go, Amos? Where would they take my boy?"

Amos wiped at the wetness upon his face and took a deep breath. "Ralph would rather hustle someone for easy money than do any hard work to make a living. I'd say he's gone back to the life he knows best."

"Why would he take Joey with him?"

Amos spoke in a quiet, defeated tone. "I'd say that wasn't Ralph's idea. It was Millie's."

John paced around the automobile, clenching and unclenching his fists, turning one way and then the other. *Think! Just try to think. There has to be some way we can find Joey.*

He went back to Amos and asked, "Did you go to the police?"

"Not yet. I was hoping that by some chance Ralph and Millie were here, that maybe I'd missed seeing them on the road…"

John stomped away from his daughter and father-in-law, distancing himself while incoherent thoughts battered his mind. He looked off in the distance, southward, in the direction of the city that was probably now claiming his youngest son as one of its residents, and knew in his heart Amos was right. The knowing robbed him of breath and chilled him in spite of the oppressive mid-summer heat. A swelling lump in John's throat threatened to choke him.

Four-year-old Joey was in a city swarming with ruthless, desperate people who were fighting for a living in a world half-empty of jobs and hope. Until now, John thought he was strong and capable and that he could weather the storm of economic depression as well as anyone of meager means, but Joey's disappearance was a blow he never anticipated. He wondered how he could ever recover from it. Raw fear insisted that his wife wouldn't. *This will kill Velma! It will kill her!*

John looked around him, at the farm and garden and mechanic work that were his family's means of survival. In his panicking mind, it seemed they were also making his family prisoners of the hard times. They could not spend their meager earnings to launch a vast search for Joey when a third of every cream check was going to the bank to satisfy a loan. He could not leave this place to go in search of his boy as the livelihood of all of them depended on his diligent overseeing of everything. Every hand was needed to help with the work if the family was going to keep food on the table and a roof over their heads. John could seek the help of the police, but unless the police could find Joey or Ralph and Millie brought him home, John realized he might never see his son again.

A wave of hopelessness reduced him to sobs. Little Joey was in Chicago and Chicago might as well be a million miles away.

Chapter Two

For the tenth time, John, *calm down!* We're not going to accomplish anything if we can't get an accurate description of these people." The police officer took a deep breath and rested his arms on the kitchen table. He took another glance around the house he had just scoured for clues and then in a lower voice asked, "John, do you have a picture of Joey or Ralph or Millie?"

John shook his head and sobbed. "I never bought a camera. I didn't think it was important."

Amos rested a reassuring hand on John's forearm. "John, Bea and I had a camera. We took pictures of Joey at his birthday party. Remember? There were three or four of Joey. Ralph and Millie were there and they were in one of the pictures."

John sighed with relief, but it was short-lived. More anxious thoughts surfaced. "They're in our bedroom. I… I don't know where… I can't go look for them or Velma will find out…"

The officer looked quizzically at John and then at Amos.

Before the man could question them, Amos blurted, "My daughter is not well. She doesn't know about this yet."

The policeman nodded as though he understood and scrawled some notes on the paper in front of him. Amos turned his attention back to John.

"Irma can find them."

"What?"

"Irma is in and out of the bedroom all the time, tending to Velma. Velma would think nothing of it if Irma was to put clothes away in a drawer or straighten something in the wardrobe. If Irma doesn't already know where those pictures are, I'm sure she can find them."

To the police officer, Amos added, "We'll get some photographs to you as soon as we can. Maybe yet today."

"Good. Now let's get some descriptions."

John let Amos do most of the talking. The officer methodically wrote down every detail and only paused when Ralph was being described.

"This sounds familiar," the officer said. "A suspect in one of our unsolved robberies was portrayed this same way."

John and Amos looked at one another and then Amos lowered his eyes. He told the man across the table, "My son-in-law was in trouble in Chicago. I had hoped since he moved up here and got a job that he would settle down and make an honest living. I guess that was too much to hope for."

The three men sat quietly, each with their own thoughts, until John asked the officer, "What are you going to do to find my boy?"

"Like Amos said, there are no signs of forced entry or struggles anywhere in this house. The neighbors saw Ralph and Millie drive away with the boy and being they didn't bring him home or return here, we have to assume that they kidnapped him. We'll notify police in surrounding communities and states and we'll ask those in the Chicago area to be on especially close watch."

The officer gathered his notes and rose to leave. "I'll get going. The sooner I get back to Rice Lake, the sooner I can make telephone calls and get other police forces on this case. I'll let you know as soon as we learn anything, John."

This case... John cringed at the words. *My missing son is "a case."* He sat in stunned silence and watched the man go. *Is that all?* John wondered. *You'll tell other policemen. You'll let me know if you learn anything. Can't you give me any more hope than that? Any hope at all?*

"Irma, what are you doing?"

Irma didn't pause in her work. "I'm dusting, Ma. It's been so dry and windy, there's dust all over everything."

Her mother sniffed. "You're just stirring it around. You're not getting rid of it."

"You're right, Ma. I'll take some of your things outside and clean them off."

Irma had been taught at a young age how to wield a feather duster. Her exuberance in cleaning her mother's room was a deliberate plot to conjure up an excuse and access the items on her mother's bedside table. While her mother rocked her chair to a soft creaking rhythm, Irma deftly rounded up an armload of books and knickknacks and framed photographs and exited the room.

At the kitchen table, she set the items down in front of her father and grandfather, then extracted her mother's Bible from the pile and flipped open the front cover, revealing the sought-after pictures. Irma had known exactly where they were and set them before her father within a few minutes of his asking for them. He lifted one with a trembling hand and stared at it through mist-laden eyes.

"I'll take them to town, John," Grandpa whispered. "If you leave now, at supper time, Velma might suspect something is wrong."

John nodded his assent. Grandpa slipped the precious pictures into his pocket and quietly left the house.

"Where is Grandpa going?" Irma's younger sister Shirley asked as she came out of the pantry. "I'll have supper ready in less than an hour."

John quickly made up an excuse. "He's taking a machine part over to Schneider's for me. He'll be back."

John rose from his chair. It was his habit to go into the bedroom to check on Velma sometime in the afternoon. He had not done so yet today. Her grandfather had started his car and Irma worried that her mother might notice when the vehicle motored down the driveway. What if her mother questioned what was going on? More lies would be told. When would the chain of untruths stop?

Irma held her breath and silently begged her father to go into the bedroom to distract her mother. At last, he squared his shoulders, took a deep breath, and put his hand on the doorknob.

Exhaling her pent-up air, Irma turned back to the disarray that covered the kitchen table. She suddenly had a good amount of extra cleaning to do and had to get it done before supper.

"Where is my little boy? Didn't my father bring him home?"

The pleading voice was weak and high-pitched, unlike the boisterous alto tones that burst from Velma when she was healthy. John cringed. He hated seeing his wife this way, with her thick dark hair cast carelessly upon an uncommonly pasty-colored face. Protruding cheekbones marred her once fleshy, round, rosy cheeks and her lively dark eyes had become listless. She was clad in a faded housecoat, sitting in a creaking rocker in the corner of their darkened bedroom. The place reeked like a sick room. John found it hard to draw a breath in the stifling confines, partly because the oppressive heat and feel of the place nauseated him, more so because of the dark secret weighing so heavily upon him.

"Your sister wasn't home," he blurted. "No one was home. Their car was gone."

Velma raised her chin and glared at him. "Father should

have waited for them. I want my Joey back home. I want all my children home."

"Now? Lillian is minding the Jensen's young ones. Phillip and Harvey are tending the cows..."

John stopped speaking and drew a long breath, trying to stifle a wave of anger rising within him. He fought the urge to reprimand his wife for being ungrateful and demanding when everyone else in the house was doing their utmost. While she lived as a troubled recluse in a dark, smelly room, her children moved stealthily through the house, terrified of disturbing their mother lest she lapse into another bout of weeping. They avoided their mother, just as John avoided coming to the house more than was needful. It was easier to be lost in work, to push his weary body to the limit, to sleep alone on the ground, rather than face the strange mental anguish that was overtaking his wife.

John swallowed hard, choked down the harsh words that nearly erupted and asked, "Is there anything I can get for you?" He asked it politely enough, yet his hopes were that she would decline his offer. He wanted to escape the foul room and return to his shop, his haven.

Velma said nothing. She turned her face sideways and her dark profile cast an eerie shadow upon the drawn shade.

John turned to go.

"John?"

He stopped.

"Where is Joey?"

"I don't know."

He shrugged casually as he said it, hoping Velma would not detect his inner fears. He wondered what would happen if he told her the truth.

I can't tell her. I can't face her with it. We don't really know where Ralph and Millie are. They might have gone on a vacation, although I don't know how they could afford such a thing. We'll hear from them in the next few days and find out what's going on. Then I'll tell Velma - after the worry is gone. The rampant thoughts and excuses flowed, yet John knew in his heart the worry was not going to go away. It was only beginning. He felt sick to his stomach.

"I'll check back with you in a while. I've got to get back to work."

John hastened out of the room and closed the door. He sucked in a deep breath that caught in his throat when he realized Irma was standing in the kitchen glaring at him. Without saying a word or drawing her sister Shirley's attention to the dire situation, she let her father know that she didn't like keeping such a secret. She seemed to know without asking that neither he nor her grandfather had uttered a word to her mother or anyone else about Joey's unknown whereabouts.

John stared back at his daughter, hoping to convey with a slight shake of his head and his woeful look what he was feeling inside. *I can't tell her yet. This hurt is too fresh and it's tearing me apart. I just can't bear to hold anyone else up right now, Irma.*

As he walked out of the house toward his dingy, grease-smelling shop, he thought about how strange it was that he found his greatest comfort in a disarranged, messy shed. In this, his refuge, he could fix things. He had the tools, means, and know-how. In that house there was an aching heart and bitter mind that he could not remedy. John's back was strong, yet he felt so weak. He could work all day and far into the night and do it day after day, but he could not face the abhorrent mental illness that was gripping Velma. It scared him as nothing else ever had in his life - until now.

God, when is this torment going to end? Why are you doing this to us?

John halted his mental ranting against God. He had no fight left in him and he saw no profit in quarreling with a being who gave him no answers. He fingered one of his wrenches and thought about the knowing look that Irma cast toward him. She was nearly seventeen years old, small in size and serious in temperament. Unlike her grandfather, who usually hid his innermost feelings, Irma was forthright in speech and let others know what was on her mind. She did not shy away from confrontation as her father did and the hard times did not drive her to sick despair as they did her mother. Somehow, though the world around them seemed senseless, Irma maintained a confidence that her elders lacked. John wondered if his little Irma might be the strongest person in the house.

Chapter Three

"That devil wind." Amos muttered the words as he pulled a damp and dirtied handkerchief from the back pocket of his overalls in order to mop sweat from his brow. Leaning on the handle of the hoe, he regarded the withering landscape from under the brim of his tattered straw hat. Each day the breezes came, hot and dry across the land. Clouds holding no promise of rain drifted lazily overhead, casting careless spots of shadow that provided no relief from the heat. It was getting to be a miserably hot and dry summer.

"Are you all right, Amos? Maybe it's time you got a drink of water and sat a spell."

"I'll sit after I get the rest of this row hoed."

While he appreciated his son-in-law's concern, Amos also felt a stab of resentment. He had survived just fine without John's help for seven decades and might be doing as well now if hadn't been for the stock market crash and the country's hardships. The Chicago store that he and his wife Beatrice had run for years began to fail after the crash, as did Beatrice's health. They moved to the quiet countryside of northern Wisconsin hoping to fare better outside of the city.

Amos had had no intention of intruding upon Velma and her family. He purchased an old farmhouse several miles from John and Velma and started a little garden there. His plan was to help the Connors on their farm if and when he felt like it, but Beatrice's health failed rapidly and Amos could not give her proper care. Their house was let out to Ralph and Millie, whom he had been encouraging to get out of Chicago. Amos moved with the ailing Beatrice into a lean-to addition on John and Velma's big house, where Velma and her daughters could help with Beatrice's care. When Beatrice passed away, Velma begged her father not to leave and Amos' temporary stay with Velma's family turned into a more permanent one.

Now that Millie and Ralph were gone and his house was no longer occupied, Amos toyed with the idea of moving back there. Velma and John had seven mouths to feed. *Six, with Joey gone.* Amos sometimes told himself they didn't really need his help around the place, since four of the children were over ten years old and capable workers. But he and the family knew that if it weren't for Amos' diligent efforts in the garden, there would be a far smaller vegetable crop to sustain them throughout the long, harsh winter.

You independent old fool, he reprimanded himself. *Beatrice is gone. If you weren't here with your grandkids, you'd be living alone in that old house and hating every minute of it. You trusted Ralph and Millie to live there and to care for Joey and you'd spend all your time chewing yourself out about the way things went wrong. You'd waste away like Bea did.*

Amos tried to shake off the hurt that came with every thought of his grandson. Three more days had slipped by. The police had found no clues about Joey's fate, but they had learned that there was money missing from Ralph's workplace. While at the police station, Amos used their telephone to make calls to acquaintances in Chicago. He had also written numerous letters, knowing that the long wait for replies was going to fuel his agony. He wondered if his efforts would do any good.

As he stuffed the sweat-dampened hankie back into his pocket, Amos surveyed the countryside around him. Arching trees edged pastureland and fields of grain that lay patchwork-like across gently rolling hills. Intense heat, unusual in this part of the country, brushed a brown pallor of drought atop each slope. It had not yet claimed the deeper lands, but even those were struggling. Their vibrant green was paling more each day, but this land had had enough rain to give the farmers a bit of hope.

"What are you thinking about, Amos?"

Amos regarded John for a moment. He didn't offer all of his thoughts, especially those misgivings about whether Joey would ever be found.

"Thinking that we have a better chance of surviving here than in a lot of the country," Amos offered. "The crops don't look as green as we'd like, but it looks like there will be something to harvest."

"For a man who spent most of his life in the city, you sure are a natural farmer…and you're right. We can keep food on the table and a roof over our heads. That's more than some folks can do. Plenty of them are ending up at the poor farm."

"I wish I could pull more of my share of the weight around here."

"You spend hours a day in this garden. If it weren't for you, Amos, I don't know what we'd eat come winter. You know Irma can't keep up with all the housework since Velma…"

John left off talking about his wife. Amos wished he would have finished what he was about to say, but politely diverted the subject to ease John's discomfort.

"It sounds like several of the neighbors are sharing more and more of their goods and their work in order to get by. Have you given any thought to joining in?"

"Sure. We've always shared in the threshing and corn husking and apple peeling and such. Sharing the feed and the work might be best in the long run. If we don't get some decent rain pretty soon, we'll all be in sorrier straights than we are now."

"Are you holding back because of Velma?"

Amos blurted it out. His decision to do so was sudden, but he needed to let out what he had been bottling up inside. For him, it was time to stop sweeping dirt under the rug, even if it might upset his son-in-law.

John uttered a deep sigh, stopped hoeing, and wiped at his damp face as Amos had done.

"I don't know what's gotten into her," John said softly. "When she isn't crying, she's sleeping. She won't tell me what's bothering her. She won't take care of the baby. She won't help with the housework. The doctor can't seem to help her and I can't either."

Amos had no intention of butting into the lives of John's family members, but his daughter's condition was lying heavier on his heart each day. He felt relieved at the opportunity to finally confide in John.

"I thought Velma was still grieving over her mother's dying, but Bea's been gone for months. You know, a man can do a lot of thinking when he's alone out here in the garden. I see how much baby Dorothy looks like Joey. It might be that seeing Dorothy reminds Velma that Joey isn't here. When Velma talks, she says things about the family not being together."

John chopped idly at the hard ground with his hoe, saying nothing and doing little damage to the weeds while Amos mustered the courage to try to address the real problem. He didn't like admitting he might be part of the cause of his daughter's grief. It was a confession he had shoved aside for a long time. But Velma's very life seemed to be slipping away, just as Beatrice's had. Maybe he could help stop it.

"You know, John, when we were in Chicago we lived in a fine house and I was able to give Beatrice and our girls a lot of nice things. They lived a pretty comfortable life. When the market crashed, I lost a lot of money. I never told Bea because I knew she would worry, but she worried anyway and the worrying made her sick."

"There's no money around here for fine things," John blurted in self-defense. "If Velma won't go out of the house because she might have to wear a flour sack dress or because her shoes are getting shabby, that's *her* problem. Nobody else around here is so high-faluting."

John stopped his tirade and hung his head for a moment. Then, he swiped at his sweaty face before looking up at Amos.

"I can't help her, Amos! I just can't! Eighteen years she's lived up here in Brill. She knows I can't give her the kind of life she lived in Chicago..."

Amos interrupted. "I know that, John, and I'm not faulting you. What I'm saying is that we've got to tell her the truth. Tell her exactly how bad things are... and tell her about Joey."

"I'm scared to death of what it'll do to her."

"So am I, but I thought I could protect Bea by not telling her what we lost. In the end, keeping it a secret didn't help a thing. I'm saying that instead of letting Velma imagine the worst, tell her the truth, and let her decide for herself what she'll do with it. We can't shield her from the hurt. She's already hurting and she can't go on the way she is much longer. We've got to face that."

John quietly regarded Amos. At length, he breathed a deep sigh and nodded his head in agreement.

"No sense delaying it. I'll go tell her right now."

"I should tell her," Amos insisted. "I was the one who raised her... and Millie." Amos hung his head and confessed in a quieter tone, "I should say I provided for them. I worked long hours and left the discipline to Bea. Now Millie's taken up with Ralph... and he's a suspect in a store robbery in Rice Lake..."

His emotions rose again – the same horrible, constricting weight of guilt and dread that brought Amos to tears when he first realized Millie was gone with Joey. He drew the large hankie from his pocket, wiped at his face, and with a trembling voice choked, "Millie stole her own sister's child! It's been over a week since anyone around here has seen them. We haven't heard a word from her..."

The thought of it was almost too much for Amos to bear. He had seen a lot of hurtful things in his long life, but this was one of the worst. When John's firm hand settled upon his shoulder in a gesture of support and understanding, his sobs unleashed. Though he didn't lift his face toward his son-in-law, he sensed that John was shedding tears, too.

"It's stupid for us to stand out here in the hot sun if we're not going to get any hoeing done," John suddenly quipped. He swiped at the moisture on his face. "Let's go see if Irma's got something for us to drink."

Amos nodded his weary head and muttered, "I've had enough of gardening for the day." As the two walked down parallel rows toward the house, he added, "I sure appreciate Irma and Shirley always having a cool drink of water for me when I come in. You're doing a fine job raising those girls, John."

"I didn't raise them by myself. Velma has been a good mother. It was asking a lot of her to marry a poor farm boy, but she was willing. What she didn't know how to do, she learned. She did a good job with our family... until now."

"I'll never forget the day Velma met you," Amos said. Reminiscing about those past days eased some of his hurt and brought a smile to his face. "We came up here on a camping vacation and had an accident with the automobile. We took it to your father's shop and there you were, tinkering with an engine. Velma took one look at you and I never heard another griping word about riding for hours in a hot car to sleep on the hard ground with mosquitoes buzzing around her head. That minute, she decided there was something good about northern Wisconsin after all."

Chapter Four

S he has taken him from me, hasn't she? Millie is not giving
Joey back."

John and Amos looked at one another, surprised that Velma
perceived the reason for their sudden visit. John made no comment. He crossed the room, drew up the shade, and threw open
the window. The fresh air and sunlight offered a hint of strength
to help him complete his unsavory mission.

"Millie promised me she would bring Joey every week to
visit," Velma said. "She didn't come this week... or last. Ralph
and Millie took him away, didn't they?"

"How did you know?" John's throat tightened. His words
came out in a hoarse whisper. Tears threatened and he blinked
rapidly to dispel them.

"I knew before you did."

Velma turned. She looked first at her husband and then at
her father. John was shocked to see a hideous glaring gleam
in her eyes. He didn't know what to say, so he said nothing.

"She took my favorite little white kitten when we were children. She took it and drowned it. She said it was an accident,
but it wasn't. She had a kitten of her own. It ran out in the street
and was run over by a car. She couldn't stand to see me have
something she couldn't have. And I trusted her with my little
Joey. She begged to take care of him, you know. She *begged* me."

John stood motionless. Velma knew. She had sensed it, had
been agonizing over it, and anticipating bad news. *For how
long? Why hadn't she said anything?*

The weight of guilt pressed upon John as much as it did Velma.

"It's my fault he's gone!" he insisted. "I encouraged the arrangement. You were so sick before Dottie was born."

John had suggested that if Velma could not care for baby Dorothy, she certainly could not chase a rambunctious four-year-old around the house and Amos was pleased that Millie had offered to help her sister's family by caring for Joey for a few weeks. How wrong they had all been!

John moved to the bed and sat down heavily upon the edge of it, leaving Amos to lean upon the doorpost with a sad, bewildered look upon his face.

"Velma, is Millie going to hurt our boy?"

Velma didn't hesitate with an answer. "She doesn't have a child of her own and she loves Joey. I don't think she intends to hurt him. That's what I keep telling myself. She doesn't plan to hurt him. She just plans to keep him."

John didn't like the calm with which Velma spoke. He eyed her until the strange look in her staring eyes softened and tears brimmed upon her dark lashes.

"That's what I keep telling myself," she whispered. Her voice cracked. "She's not going to hurt him. She wants to keep him for her own."

"Velma, the police haven't been able to locate Ralph and Millie," John confessed. "Your father has been writing letters and making telephone calls to people all over Chicago. We've gotten no news yet, and no leads." Fear gripped him so hard that it felt as though it would choke him. "Velma, I don't know what to do."

Tears coursed down Velma's cheeks in streams. Her lower lip quivered and she begged, "Just hold me."

———————⌒⌒)—————————

"The way you're yanking on that bolt, you'll break it off, and then we'll have an awful time getting this radiator off."

John regarded the grease-blackened wrench that lay in the grip of his strong hand and cast a tentative smile at Lloyd. "I guess I am taking my frustrations out on your tractor. I'm supposed to be fixing it, not making it worse."

"That's right. I can bust 'em up just fine without anybody's help," Lloyd said with a laugh. "Did I tell you how I managed to wreck this thing?"

John ran his hand across the Twin City's branch-impaled radiator and shook his head. "You didn't tell me. I heard it from a neighbor when I went to the store a couple days ago."

"Word does get around. Never done such a thing before, hopping off a tractor without making sure it was out of gear. Bumped the clutch and away she went. Didn't catch the thing until it ran square into that tree and stalled."

John surveyed the wreckage around him and quipped, "It looks to me like it ran over half the farm first. You're lucky you're alive to tell about it. Does this thing go so fast you couldn't catch up to it?"

"Oh, I could have caught it if I didn't have the side rake behind it. I dodged out of the way of the rake and tripped and fell. Kinda sprained my ankle."

Lloyd laughed again and adjusted his cap to its typical sideways cant upon his head. He was usually smiling and always fidgeting. That bothered John today. He wasn't in the mood for the man's robust energy and constant chatter, but the machine was needful since there was more hay to make and threshing time was nearing. John had to get the tractor fixed.

"I had an awful mess," Lloyd jabbered. "The old Twin City ripped out a length of fence four rods long and it didn't take ten minutes for the cows to find out about it. She ran over a post at the edge of the hog pen and let them out. Then she ran through the garden. Did I ever get in hot water over that..."

The incessant creaking of the nearby windmill, driven by

the hot wind, increased John's irritation. He made a pretense of listening to Lloyd's high-pitched, animated voice, as he applied his wrench to another bolt and let his mind drift back to the hurt buried deep in his soul.

John cussed himself out again and again for letting Millie take Joey when it was time for Velma to give birth. Joey was lively and naughty, yet Irma, Shirley and Lillian could have managed their chores and housework with him around. But Millie was adventurous and fun-loving and Joey adored her. She had taken good care of him. Each time she brought him for a visit, he was clean and well-dressed, rambunctious and healthy, and flourishing to greater degree than his own children. Ralph should have been more of a concern. He had few good virtues. The man had little interest in anyone but himself and surely wasn't much interested in having a little boy around. *Now he has Joey. Why did he take Joey with him?*

John's biggest fear was that Ralph had tired of the child and, instead of bringing him home where he belonged, had hurt him… or disposed of him. Ralph had a mean streak that didn't often show up when he was around Millie's family, but Ralph had said things that concerned John. Now John learned that Amos had the same bad feelings about Ralph. *Why did I let Joey go? Why?*

"John?"

Lloyd called his name a couple times before John responded.

"Sorry, Lloyd. What did you say?"

"I asked if you've decided to work with the rest of us."

John had participated in discussions about how farm families could help one another survive when the income from their agricultural products plummeted and the dry weather took a toll on their crops. He knew it was probably the right thing to do, but he felt so burdened of late that he couldn't even think about being helpful to others. John mumbled a lame excuse.

"I don't know if I can do my fair share, Lloyd. If the boys were older, they could help more…"

"Your boys will be a big help! They can herd the cattle when they forage in the swamps and you pull your weight as good as anybody. I ain't as young as I used to be, so I'm thinking on taking in an orphan to help get my work done. One of my cousins is getting one."

John cast a wry smile in Lloyd's direction and made an attempt at returning to his work, but Lloyd wouldn't let the matter rest.

"Look, John, we all have a lot of struggles right now. It doesn't matter to us that you don't have the tractors some of us do. You've got a good sturdy team of work horses and the machines you've got get the work done. That's what counts. You're one of the best mechanics we've got in these parts and we need someone who can forge parts out of whatever is lay-ing around."

Lloyd seemed to sense he was not convincing John. He tried another approach.

"John, we all want to be able to supply for our families on our own, but we can't be prideful at a time like this. Folks are losing their farms and homes. This mess isn't our doing and it's too big for us to fix, but we *can* survive it if we all pull together."

Lloyd had unknowingly cut to the heart of the problem and John didn't like it. He knew he should become part of a group that would share their means with one another. He knew he needed them and that he could do them good in return, but if he joined, the others would find out how his family was falling apart. Admitting such a thing stung his prideful heart.

"What's wrong, John?"

John swallowed hard, trying to dispel the lump that stopped up his throat, and then turned to his neighbor and blurted out the truth that was wrenching at his very soul. "Joey's gone."

"What do you mean, gone?"

"Amos went to Ralph and Millie's house a couple of weeks ago to bring my boy back home. They're not there. Ralph and Millie moved out and took the boy with them."

Lloyd's face registered shock. He seemed to be at a loss for words, but not for long.

"Are you sure? Did you ask the neighbors?"

"They saw Ralph and Millie put the boy and some suitcases in the car and then drive away. No one has seen them since and we haven't heard anything from them."

"Did you talk to the police?"

"Yes, but there's little they can do if Ralph took Joey to Chicago."

"Chicago!"

"That's where he's from. And you know that's where Millie grew up."

Lloyd, being a distant relative to Amos, knew well where Millie had grown up. He tipped his hat back and scratched the top of his balding head.

"What are you going to do, John?"

"All I can do is wait and hope Ralph and Millie were called away and left a note we didn't find or maybe sent a letter we haven't gotten."

"And pray."

John turned his face back to the damaged tractor. *Pray? That hasn't done me any good. Everything is falling apart around me. I can barely make ends meet. I can't keep my family together and my wife has lost all hope.*

An aching question swept through John's mind—one that he couldn't ignore. *Am I losing all hope, too?*

Chapter Five

Irma rocked little Dorothy and fed her the bottle. She found it a pleasant task as it was her only opportunity to sit and relax during the day. It made her feel very grown up and responsible to know she was capable of doing so much to feed and care for the family and house. However, Irma wearied of coaxing her mother to eat and get out of bed during the day. It was one thing to care for a helpless infant and feed a hungry family. It was another to tend to an uncooperative adult.

Rocking Dorothy gave Irma time to ponder her mother's lethargy. A neighbor lady said she would snap out of it and that melancholy sometimes came over a woman after birthing a babe, but it had been over six weeks. Her mother looked more harried every day, even though she was getting far more rest than anyone else in the house. Irma had never known someone to sleep as much as her mother did, unless they were very old… or very sick.

Irma hoped, as her father and grandfather did, that when her mother learned about Joey's disappearance, something would change. But there seemed to be little difference in Velma's sad demeanor. She didn't seem any worse, but neither was she improved. Irma wondered what her mother's condition would be if the hurtful ordeal had been talked about right away, but folks in her family held secrets very dear. Unfortunately, they seemed to be sorely burdened by knowing what they did.

Grandpa pulled the screen door open and hobbled into the house. His back was stooped, his leathery face flushed pink from working in the heat. Irma thought he looked more aged than ever.

"I'd sure like to see it rain and cool things down, but it might as well hold off 'til the threshing's done," he said. "Heat like this, if it does get to raining, will likely bring bad weather. We don't need to lose what little grain we've got to wind and hail."

"We'd be hard put to get through winter if we lose our grain." Irma spoke softly, for baby Dorothy's eyes were closed in slumber and she didn't want to waken her.

"When will they be threshing here?" she asked.

"Your pa figures it will be a couple weeks." Her grandfather seemed to sense her consternation. "Irma, don't worry about how we're going to feed the threshing crew. You won't be doing it alone. The other womenfolk know you have your hands full, especially now that Shirley works sometimes over at the Miller's."

Irma spoke softly so her mother could not overhear from the nearby room. Amos had to lean toward her to discern what she was saying.

"I just wish Ma could help. The medicine from the doctor hasn't done her any good..."

"There's no medicine for what's ailing her, Irma," her grandfather whispered back. "The doctor can't fix her."

"Is she dying?"

Irma had wondered about it for a long time. She wanted an honest answer. At first, she thought she wasn't going to get one from her grandfather, for he was looking askance at the closed bedroom door, not uttering a word.

"She's giving up on living," he finally muttered. "Sometimes a person gets to feeling so sorrowful, they make themselves sick."

"Is that what happened to Grandma?"

Irma had been determined not to burst into tears as her mother so often did, but keeping the mist out of her eyes and the tightening from her throat was impossible when she recalled the sad manner of her grandmother's suffering and passing.

"Your grandma had pains and ailments that a lot of people live with for a long time. She didn't fight them or suffer through them. She fell to them." Grandpa's eyes misted a bit also. He hesitated, then added, "Misery can be a very deadly companion."

Irma had resented the way her grandmother griped and moaned about things. She had thought the woman was ungrateful and that she just wanted attention. *Did Grandma invite misery into her life? Is that what Ma is doing?*

"Grandpa, do you think Ma would get better if we got Joey back?"

Amos hesitated again and a strange look passed over his face. Irma couldn't comprehend what he was thinking.

"I think it would help your ma a lot to see Joey and know he is safe. In the meantime, we'll just keep doing what we can. Something is bound to change."

Irma nodded her head in agreement. She knew about the frequent letters Grandpa mailed to Chicago. He was doing what he could to try to locate her brother, but she had a strange feeling Grandpa was up to something more than letter writing.

───────❧───────

The engine sputtered to life with Lloyd's first attempt at starting his tractor. The grin of delight on his face made John chuckle.

"She runs better than she ever did since I bought her, John!" the proud tractor owner announced.

"Glad to hear it. Now, before you run off with it, let me get the last of the tinwork straightened and bolted on."

Lloyd shut the motor off. He hopped down from the Twin City and came around to where John held the hood that needed work.

"I sure appreciate the good job you do, John. I'll get you paid in full as soon as I can."

"I know you will."

"Will you take a pig home as part payment? He'll be big enough to butcher come fall."

John eyed the herd of swine in the nearby pen. They weren't worth much of anything at the market and John didn't need more work. He had hoped Lloyd would pay him in cash for his efforts, but John did have a craving for crisp-fried side pork, so he nodded in agreement.

"I guess we have enough garden waste to fatten a hog, but I can't take it home until I've got a pen fixed up."

"If it's easier for you, we can truck the garden waste over here. I don't want to put you out or make so much work for you that you can't fix my machinery."

John chuckled. "There is one last thing I'm going to fix up as soon as I get this tractor finished and that's that fool squawking windmill. How long has it been since you've greased that thing?"

Lloyd laughed. "I don't recall. I've been meaning to climb up there and do it, but time keeps getting away on me. I'm so used to the noise that I don't even pay attention to it any more."

"I'll grease it before I leave today."

"No, I'll go take care of it right now. It'll give me something to do besides getting in your way."

John smiled to himself as Lloyd walked toward his ramshackle tool shed. It seemed Lloyd couldn't resist spending time socializing. If there was someone to talk to, Lloyd was there doing it. But he had a habit of standing in the wrong place, forcing John to work around him.

After a few minutes of clattering around in the little lopsided building, Lloyd emerged and sauntered past John with a pail of grease and a couple of wrenches.

"Lloyd? You don't need wrenches to grease your windmill," John quipped.

"It just so happens there's a loose rung on the ladder and I'm going to replace the bolts with some good sturdy ones," Lloyd stated. "I may not be good at fixing tractors, but I know how to tighten bolts."

He laughed as he walked toward his windmill and set the brake. The squawking stopped, leaving John to work in blessed peace.

Pounding out the last of the dents in the tinwork took only a few minutes. John lifted the gray hood and fit it carefully over the engine, aligned the bolt holes, and began fastening it down. This Twin City was the first John had ever worked on. It seemed to be a good sturdy tractor and John liked the sound of the powerful 4-cylinder engine. *Lloyd said it has thirty-five horsepower. It will be interesting to see how the belt drive does under load when we hook it up to that big separator.* He eyed the wide cleated steel wheels. They were certainly capable of propelling the Twin City over rough ground – and a lot of objects in its path. John thought Lloyd was pretty lucky to have a cousin who had started up a dealership and was willing to give his relatives good deals on used equipment.

Rhythmic light tapping sounded above him, telling John that Lloyd must have found the loose rung and was pounding a new bolt into the old hole. Although Lloyd made light of his abilities, John knew the man to be a capable carpenter. He just didn't lend himself to overusing that skill, as the run-down appearance of some of the buildings proclaimed. *I guess he just needs motivation. When he thought I was going to go grease his windmill, he decided it was something he could do...*

Snap! Grating metal. Lloyd's sharp intake of breath and then a fearful cry. John instantly became alert to the sounds, but before he could urge his feet to move, Lloyd came crashing down. He hit several steps, bounced off the bottom rung, and sprawled in a patch of weeds at the base of the windmill.

John ran on rubbery legs, terrified of what he might find as he parted the shoulder-high patch of nettles. He knelt by Lloyd's side and knew immediately that he wasn't breathing.

Suddenly, Lloyd caught his wind. He gasped for air. After several gulps, he managed to whisper, "Knocked the wind outta me."

As he drew in a couple more breaths, Lloyd winced. "I'm hurt."

"I'm not surprised," John exclaimed. "I thought for a minute you were dead."

Lloyd closed his eyes and took more breaths – shallow ones drawn very cautiously.

"You probably broke some ribs," John said as he made an assessment of Lloyd's wounds. "Your right leg is broken for sure. I'll go tell Gertie what happened and we'll get you to the doctor."

"John, this isn't good," Lloyd gasped. "Gertie and I don't need doctor bills right now. The threshing… the farm work…"

"Don't worry about it, Lloyd. You've got several more hogs. Maybe the doctor will take a couple off your hands as payment for fixing you up."

John made the comment with a wry smile. Lloyd tried to smile back, but had to grit his teeth against the pain. "I can't pull my share of the weight like the rest of the farmers. How am I going to get the work done? I need to put up wood for winter…"

"We'll get it done," John assured him. "But we might have to use that fancy tractor of yours to do it."

Chapter Six

"I should have climbed up there and fixed that windmill," John said at the breakfast table. "Lloyd is so clumsy. I should have known he'd fall."

"He's been up and down that thing a hundred times," Amos argued as he slathered a piece of day-old bread with lard. "He knew full well things were getting loose, didn't he? He should have tightened those bolts long ago. You got no call to blame yourself."

"I blame myself for feeling sorry for him and opening up my big mouth and telling him not to worry about his chores and putting up wood. I told him we would help him out."

"Other folks are pitching in too, and the boys are more than happy to do chores over there. Gertie always has a fine treat for them."

Fourteen-year-old Phillip stopped eating his oatmeal and bread long enough to join the conversation. "Miss Gertie gave me and Grandpa doughnuts when we took slop to the hogs. If she wasn't expecting company, she might have sent a whole sack of 'em home with us."

Irma listened to the conversation with a twinge of resentment. *Gertie Schneider doesn't have anyone but Lloyd to tend to or cook for. The neighbors are helping with Lloyd's work and feeding them is the least she can do.*

When she was finished with her own breakfast, Irma left the table. Shirley glanced at her with a questioning look since Irma usually partook in the conversation and lingered over a cup of sweet hot water tea on a Sunday morning. The others seemed to take no notice when Irma disappeared.

She hastened up the steep, narrow stairs to the upper room she shared with Shirley and Lillian. There Irma exchanged her faded housedress for her newest flour sack dress – a fine, flowery print that her mother made for her a year ago. She smoothed her wavy light-brown hair and studied her image in the mirror that rested on the bureau.

Her pale green eyes were too wide-set for Irma's liking and the dark shadows under them tainted her smooth sun-kissed complexion. Her lips were thin and straight, giving her a serious look. She would have liked to add some color to them, as some women did, but knew her father would not have any of that. She would be hard pressed to get out of the house unscathed as it was.

As she moved toward the bedroom door, Irma wondered how her father would react to her resolve. She drew a deep breath and slipped out of the room, determined to find out. She knew the soft clopping of her shoes on the stairs was sure to alert her family that something was going on for it was her habit to go barefoot except in the worst of weather. When she appeared at the bottom of the stairs, her father was gazing in her direction with a curious expression on his face.

"I'm going to church," she announced before he could ask. "I'll wash up the breakfast dishes when I get back."

Her father and grandfather made no comment. Irma hastened toward the door.

"Can I go with you?"

It was Shirley who asked. Irma was at once relieved and disheartened. Dare she and Shirley leave baby Dorothy at home with the menfolk and eight-year-old Lillian? *It might be best if I did. If they need help, maybe Ma will take some initiative to take care of her own baby.*

"What about Dottie?" her father challenged. "Who's going to take care of her?"

"If no one else around here can mind her, I'll take her with me!" The words came out more harshly than Irma intended. She didn't want the struggle of lugging the baby to church, but she would do it if she had to. Even if she walked in late, she was going to go.

"What made you decide to go to church all of a sudden?"

Her father asked the question calmly, but Irma still felt as though she was being confronted. She was ready with an answer that revealed what had been stirring in her heart for quite some time. When she spoke them, her words were firm and measured.

"I'm not going to sit here and die like others are doing. People are dying, hopes and dreams are dying, and our faith is dying. But I'm not going to give up. I'm going to hold onto my dreams and I'm going to keep my faith. The Bible says God will provide what we need and I'm going to believe it."

Before anyone could respond or criticize, she fled out the door and started down the dusty road. She was halfway down the driveway, shaken yet elated for overcoming a dreaded moment, when Irma realized she left the baby and Shirley behind. She didn't go back for them.

Irma had walked over a mile when a car pulled up beside her. She kept her eyes straight ahead and her feet pacing the dusty lane, unwilling to face any member of her family that might have come to demand something of her. If they did, they were going to get another dose of her pent-up frustration.

I'm not staying in that house all day every day anymore! I don't get to go to town for supplies. I don't even get to go to the pasture to fetch cows! I go outside to wash clothes and hang them on the line. I go to the pump to fetch water. I go to the garden to gather vegetables. Today, I'm going to church!

Irma continued her march and her internal ranting until Shirley rolled down the window of her grandfather's coupe and asked if she wanted a ride. It was then that Irma cast a sideways glance. Shirley rode in the front passenger seat with baby Dorothy in her lap and Lillian sat in the back seat. The girls' faces were freshly scrubbed, their hair neatly combed and they had donned their best clothing. Grandpa sat behind the wheel with a mischievous smirk on his face. He had traded his patched overalls for a fine pair of trousers and a freshly pressed white shirt that hadn't been out of the wardrobe since Grandma's funeral. He was clean-shaven and his hair, which was usually bushy and unruly, had been slicked back. Irma was struck by the sight of the cheery, expectant faces that stared at her.

"Are you going to stand there looking at us or are you going to get in so we can get to church on time?" Grandpa asked with mock sternness.

Irma smiled broadly and climbed into the seat next to Lillian. As soon as she was settled, Grandpa put the car in gear.

Irma's heart raced with excitement. There would be neighbors to talk to. There would be singing and a fine sermon that would surely help put her dreary existence into perspective.

Too long, Irma thought, her family had focused on their physical needs and neglected their spiritual ones. Their church attendance had dwindled and so had their fellowship with their neighbors. Being reclusive and secretive about her mother's illness hadn't gained them anything. It had bred more sorrow and strain. Perhaps now, with the decision of some of them to be more social, they were getting back onto the right path. And maybe this day would mark the start of something new for all of them.

"It is so good to see you again, Irma."

It was Lloyd's wife, Gertie, who approached Irma after the church service. As she tickled Dorothy under the chin, she said, "Your brother Phillip told me your mother is still not feeling well. I'm so sorry to hear it."

Irma changed the subject and asked, "How is Mr. Schneider? Pa was really scared when he fell. He thought he was busted up a lot worse than he was."

"Lloyd is getting along, but he is not a good patient. You would think a broken leg and cracked ribs would keep him down, but he can't sit still. Until he learns to take it easy, he'll continue to be sore and miserable."

Several other women stopped to greet Irma.

"This is little Dorothy? How adorable! May I hold her?" one asked.

Irma relinquished her littlest sister and cast a sideways glance toward Shirley, who had passed Dorothy off as soon as they entered the church. Shirley was now freely mingling with other mid-teen youths, leaving Irma to mind Dorothy and converse with older women.

"How are things going with you, Gertie?" one of the women asked.

"We're doing okay. We have wonderful neighbors and a young man who has come to help us. Irma's father, bless his heart, has been so good to us. And do you know that Velma is *still* not feeling well?"

Gertie leveled a look of genuine concern toward Irma. "How old is Dorothy?"

"Near two months."

"Your mother should be up and around by now! Has the doctor been by to see her?"

The subject of her mother's ill health was something Irma didn't relish discussing with everyone, but she was determined to be polite and ladylike as her mother taught her, so she replied to the question.

"The doctor gave her some tonic, but it hasn't helped her."

"Poor woman," an elderly neighbor remarked.

The women began talking of baby-birthing maladies they had overcome and the conversation made Irma uncomfortable. She turned her attention back to the young people and noticed someone standing off to the side who she didn't recollect seeing before. *Probably one of the Sutherland boys sprouting up like a weed,* she decided.

"Irma, I'm going to stop by your house this week," Gertie suddenly announced.

Irma snapped to attention. The woman quietly took Irma's arm and led her away from the other ladies. Irma was thankful for that as she didn't want to argue Gertie's plans in front of the others.

"Mrs. Schneider, I don't think Ma will be…"

"I'm not coming for a tea party, Irma. I'm concerned about your mother. Maybe some company will cheer her up or maybe she needs a friend to talk to. I know about Joey being gone and… I know how it feels to lose a son."

Irma had forgotten about the tragedy that had taken one of the Schneider's sons many years ago. She didn't really want company at the house, seeing her mother in such a sorry condition, but she didn't argue for she suddenly realized that perhaps her mother needed to see a new face once in a while. Maybe her mother had the same unspoken longing Irma had had this very morning – a longing to be loosed from drudgery and worry, and to be reassured of God's love.

"I have the makings of some fine homemade doughnuts. Maybe you and I can make some together one day."

Irma smiled at the thought of such a treat. "You would teach me how to make your good doughnuts?"

"If you're willing to learn, I will. It's the least I can do. I should not have neglected visiting you and your mother for so long. The heat has been miserable, but Lloyd and I could have come in the evening when it was cooler."

Amos left off talking to neighbors and approached the gathering of women. "Are you ready to go, Irma?" he asked.

"Yes, Grandpa."

The woman who held Dorothy gave the baby one more pat on the cheek and handed her back to Irma, who toted the infant toward the car in the steps of her grandfather. Shirley and Lillian were approaching, having come from the scattered clusters of younger people whom Irma would have liked to have visited with. Irma didn't show her disappointment and kept her silence rather than reprimand her sisters for leaving her with the baby's care, but she made a vow to herself. *Next week I'm going to make Shirley take care of Dorothy and I'm going to find somebody to talk to besides a bunch of old ladies.*

Chapter Seven

The music of Sunday's church service ran through Irma's head while she scrubbed her brother's filthiest barn clothes on the washboard. She hummed the tune of "How Firm a Foundation," which stirred her heart as it never had before. A firm foundation certainly sounded better than the uncertainty she was living with.

How firm a foundation, ye saints of the Lord, Is laid for your faith in His excellent Word! What more can He say than to you He hath said, To you, who for refuge to Jesus have fled?

Fear not, I am with thee, O be not dismayed, For I am thy God, I will still give thee aid; I'll strengthen thee, help thee, and cause thee to stand, Upheld by My gracious, omnipotent hand.

Fear, Irma considered, was perhaps the greatest problem in her home. Fear of the unknown future, fear of losing everything, fear of what might befall Joey. They had the means and know-how to grow and preserve their own food as well as to hunt and fish. The government was putting money into failing banks and giving jobs to many unemployed, but there was still a heavy load of worry and uncertainty.

Our best help comes from God, not the government, Irma determined. *He promised He would help us! We haven't gotten a lot of rain, but our garden is growing. Pa is getting lots of mechanic work. Phillip and Shirley have gotten jobs. We have all we really need, except for knowing if Joey is all right.*

Irma turned her thoughts to the last verse of the song. That one needed more pondering than the others.

When thro' fiery trials thy pathway shall lie, My grace, all sufficient, shall be thy supply; The flames shall not hurt thee, I only design thy dross to consume, and thy gold to refine.

Irma shut off the gas engine that powered the Maytag washer and began pulling diapers out of the sudsy water. As she wrung water out of the cloth, she considered the refining process. The thought of hardship refining someone gave her pause. *If living in hard times is a refining process, maybe the rest of us will be better off in the long run, but Lord, what about Ma? Isn't it hardship that's destroying her?*

Irma decided that being refined had to be a voluntary thing. If folks had enough faith in Jesus, they would let Him change them for the better. Maybe God deliberately let people go through trials to either drive them crazy or drive them to their knees. If so, it was up to each individual whether trouble terrorized them or toughened them.

Irma continued to scrub, wring water, ponder and pray. *Lord, please get rid of the dross in me and polish up the gold.*

The soft fall of footsteps behind her made Irma twirl around. She started. A slender young man stood nearby, dusty and dirty. His shirt was sweat-stained and his unkempt mop of hair was damp around his sweat-moistened brow. He carried a greasy brown paper bag in one hand and Irma thought surely he was a bum or a beggar.

"We don't have any extra food," she warned.

The young man glared at her.

"Mr. Connor has work for me."

"He's not here right now. He went to town for supplies, but we've got no work we can't do ourselves. You might as well go somewhere else to look for work."

"Mr. Connor told me to come, so I came. I'm not listening to a twelve-year-old!"

Irma slapped a diaper on the surface of the water. It made

a splat. "I am not twelve years old!" she shouted. "I'm older than you!"

"You are not!"

"I'm so close to seventeen, I can spit at it!"

"Well, I'm already seventeen! In a few months, I can go to work in a CC camp instead of on some stupid cow farm."

"You're lying! You ain't much bigger than my fourteen-year-old brother!"

The window behind her opened a crack and Irma heard her mother's weak voice.

"Irma, is something wrong?"

Irma quieted and turned toward the house, while keeping a wary eye on the young man who stood before her.

"No, ma. Nothing is wrong."

She wasn't about to tell her mother that they had a belligerent bum in the yard for her mother didn't need more worry. Irma was determined to handle this herself.

"I reckon I'll go over here and wait for Mr. Connor."

The young man strolled over to the wood pile and sat with his bag on the chopping block.

"Suit yourself," Irma mumbled. She went back to scrubbing clothes, knowing that the bum was watching her. She didn't like it one bit and kept an eye upon him in case he tried to steal something.

"Too bad you don't have work for me and you aren't going to feed me. I'll just have to eat what's in this sack. I need *something* to eat. It's been hours since I had breakfast."

He pulled a sugar-coated treat out of the paper sack and made sure Irma was watching when he took a big bite of it. Irma suddenly remembered that Mrs. Schneider had told her she was coming and that she would teach Irma how to make those very same delicious doughnuts.

"Where did you get those? Did you steal them from Mrs. Schneider?"

Irma approached the boy with a hefty stick in her hand – the one she fished clothes out of scalding water with. The young man didn't flinch. He just sat there chewing his food, looking at her with a disgusting arrogant sneer on his face.

"I didn't steal them," he said calmly. "Mrs. Schneider gave them to me to give to you and your family being she's delayed in coming here. But since I don't have anything else to eat…"

"You're the Schneider's new hired man?" Irma asked. She realized then that he was the young man who had been standing apart from the others at church – the one she couldn't identify. Feeling as though she had an advantage, Irma changed her tack. "I guess you're not really a hired man. I heard the Schneiders were getting a helper – from the orphanage in LaCrosse."

The young man glared at her. Irma felt a tinge of regret at mentioning where he came from. The words of that song she had been humming a while ago stole back through her mind: *Thy dross to consume and thy gold to refine.* Irma knew at that moment she had more dross to deal with than she cared to admit. She had treated the young man with contempt when there was no call for it.

"I guess you're not a bum like I thought you were." The words were said with more meekness than she had displayed thus far, but they came far short of the apology Irma knew she should offer. Apologies did not slide easily off her lips.

The sound of a car approaching the farmhouse brought Irma's attention to the driveway. She wiped her soapy hands on her already damp apron and approached the Schneider's vehicle.

"Good afternoon, Mrs. Schneider," Irma called.

"Good afternoon, Irma. I didn't think I would get here today, so I sent some donuts with Allen, but Lloyd is already done with his doctor visit and we have our other errands finished, so here I am. Would you like help with the wash?"

"Thank you, but I'm almost done. I just have a couple more overalls to scrub and a basket of wet stuff to hang on the line."

Gertie went round the vehicle to help Mr. Schneider. Once he was upright, Lloyd was able to navigate on his crutches. He headed toward John's shop until Irma called to him and told him her pa was in town, but due home soon. He then hobbled toward a bench under a fine, large shade tree. Allen moved toward him.

"Allen, I thought you were supposed to be helping John," Lloyd said.

"He's not here and no one has given me anything to do," the young man said, defending himself. He cast a dark look in Irma's direction.

"You were standing next to a chopping block and there's an ax laying right there. You could chop firewood until John gets here."

Without a word, Allen left the sack of doughnuts in Gertie's hands and spun around on his heel to march back to the chopping block.

"I'll go into the house and visit with your mother, if you don't mind," Mrs. Schneider said.

Irma nodded her assent and plunged her hands back into the dirty water. As she scrubbed, her gaze drifted to Mr. Schneider's helper, who was rolling up his sleeves in anticipation of hefting the splitting maul.

He's pretty skinny to be of much help doing anything around here, Irma thought.

A muffled whimper reminded Irma that Dottie was lying in a basket in the shade of the house.

"Don't be throwing any wood in this direction," she warned Allen. "There's a baby in that basket."

The young man cast a scowling gaze toward the infant and then a sly glance in Irma's direction. She could understand why he showed such a contrary attitude toward her, but why he would scowl at her cute baby sister, she couldn't comprehend. All Irma knew about him was that she didn't like the proud tilt of that boy's head and the smirk that curled his lip.

———————— ⌒⌒ ————————

With tall glasses of cool water in their hands and a platter of homemade donuts in front of them, the men settled under the gnarled shade tree for a visit.

"Allen's got some experience with field work and cattle, but he's learning about hogs the hard way," Lloyd quipped as he helped himself to a doughnut. "We tried to get one separated out for you, but the hog wasn't cooperating and Allen and Gertie couldn't handle it by themselves."

"I don't have the pen fixed up yet anyway. The boys and I will get at it in the next couple days," John said. He turned his attention to the young man. "Lloyd tells me you're from LaCrosse."

"I'm not from there. That's where I've been staying."

"You came from the orphanage?"

"Yes, sir."

The young man seemed ill at ease, so John didn't pursue further conversation with him. Lloyd didn't let the talking lapse, and while he chattered, John and Amos helped themselves to fresh-made doughnuts.

"I wrote them and asked for a helper a few weeks ago, as soon as my boy got that job up north," Lloyd said. "You know how Gertie likes to cook. There are kids in that orphanage that need food and a place to stay and we've got both. Gertie thought it would be good to have an extra hand around."

"Especially if you're going to take great pains to get out of doing your share of the work," John teased.

Lloyd seemed to take no offense for he laughed aloud at the remark, but he suddenly grew uncharacteristically sober.

"John, I don't have enough money right now to pay you for fixing my tractor. I'd like for you to use it for your own work instead of you having to do everything with your horses, but now I'm afraid I'm going to have to sell the Twin City to pay my bills. I don't know what else to do."

John expelled a long breath of air. This news wasn't unexpected, given Lloyd's circumstances, but the words still stung when leveled at a man who needed payment for doing Lloyd's repair work.

"You got some cows milking, don't you?" John asked.

"Either those old cows aren't getting enough good feed or the old DeLaval isn't separating cream like it's supposed to. The cream check barely covers the price of feed and supplies anymore. We've been getting by, but we're losing ground. And now this…" Lloyd indicated his bum, splinted leg and uttered a deep sigh. "Allen is a good, strong boy and a willing worker, but he doesn't know how to do everything around the place. I don't know how he'll manage come threshing time, if he's gotta help the crew and take care of the milking. You know Gertie isn't fond of milking cows."

John pondered the situation for a while.

"Your young stock is grazing in the swamps?"

"Or sold off, like everybody else's. I'm going to have to dry off some of the cows and turn them loose, too, if I can't afford to buy feed for 'em. The pasture is just getting too short."

John had been frugal and cautious with his money. Being content to make income from his mechanic shop, he had been slower to expand his milking herd than many of the neighbors. He had also been slower to purchase modern tractors and machinery since he was adept at keeping the old horse-drawn equipment going. Being his land was skirted by wooded hills and swamp bottom, John tended to have more pasture than many of his neighbors.

"Maybe we can put your cows with ours and my boys can milk them. Allen can help me with the field work and machinery being he's stronger than Phillip and Harvey."

"Sounds to me like we're pooling our resources."

John nodded his head. His worries about Joey certainly weren't over, but having a vision and making plans seemed to give him a measure of calm he hadn't been feeling of late. His former resolve to triumph over hardship was returning as was his determination to do what he could and control what he could. The rest he would leave for Irma and the other churchgoers to pray about.

As John continued to discuss possibilities with Lloyd and Allen, he kept a wary eye on Amos. Amos had downed his water and a generous portion of sweet treats from the platter, but for some reason the old man had become strangely silent.

Chapter Eight

Weeks had gone by and no word had come from Millie. There was little change in Velma's disposition but storms had brought rain that blessed the dry ground, easing a bit of worry. The threshing was nearly finished, the garden was yielding fine crops, and Amos had helped Irma and Shirley put the fruits of his labor into storage. Jars of fine looking canned goods lined the cellar shelves and bins were ready and waiting for the root crops that would be dug later in the fall. Now, Amos figured, was the time to do what he had in mind to do.

The mission had been on his mind for weeks. He had written letters to acquaintances in Chicago and had contacted the police there. The replies he received netted no encouraging clues as to Joey's whereabouts. Amos thought he might be better able to track down Ralph and Millie by himself instead of relying upon others to help, but the decision to go back to Chicago didn't come easy. Strangely enough, when he felt most in doubt about what he should do, it was the preacher's sermon that settled it.

It had not been Amos' habit to go to church – not since he was a young man. Church was something Velma took an interest in when she took an interest in John, for John's family was a church-going one. The preacher surely didn't know Amos would be attending that day and didn't know what Amos needed to hear, but the sermon seemed to be aimed squarely at him. The preacher had talked about God comforting us in our tribulations so we can comfort others who are in trouble but men's efforts to fix others would be in vain without God's help.

Alone in the garden, in the cool of the morning, Amos had pondered what the preacher said. If it was true, Amos' efforts to right Velma's problems were going to be futile – unless he was ready to let God have the reins. As he hoed, Amos talked to God about Velma. *Lord, I can't fix her. The only thing that might cheer her up is if Joey comes back to us. I still believe that Ralph and Millie went to Chicago. It's been on my mind for weeks to go there and try to find them myself.* Amos stopped hoeing. He leaned on the handle and confessed in a whisper, "Lord, I've made all kinds of excuses for not going, telling myself I could do just as well by asking others to help, telling myself I was needed here. Truth is, I didn't want to spend the money to go. That boy's life might be in danger and I haven't done all I could because it might cost me what little money I have. Lord, I need as much of Your help as Millie and Velma do."

Once Amos resigned himself to making the trip he started making plans. It was a long shot, finding a little boy in a city of such size, but Amos knew he had to try. The journey would be for his own good more than anyone else's.

Amos hadn't told the family of his intentions. John left the house early to work at a distant neighbor's place. The boys were doing barn chores and Shirley was gone to help cook for the threshing crew. The house was fairly quiet since Dottie was sleeping and Velma was sitting in her room. Only Irma was stirring about in the kitchen.

Packing took but a few minutes. Amos stuffed his carpetbag with clothing and then dug a folded sock from the bottom of his trunk. He pulled a wad of bills from it, counted some out, and stuffed it into his pocket. Then he walked into the farm-house kitchen. He set his bag down on the table and pressed some money into Irma's hand.

"Grandpa, what are you doing?" she asked in alarm.

"I'm taking a trip. That money is for things you and your ma and the family might need while I'm gone."

Irma looked at the fistful of money. She didn't count it, but seemed to sense that it was more than they had seen in quite some time. She didn't ask where it came from. Her concern was for her grandfather.

"Where are you going?"

"Chicago."

Irma was not as stunned by the announcement as he thought she would be.

"I was hoping someone would go and bring Joey back," she whispered. "You've been thinking about this for a long time, haven't you, Grandpa?"

"Quite a while."

"Does Pa know you're leaving?"

"No. I don't need anyone reasonable telling me that I'm wasting my time. My gut tells me I can find Joey and I've gotta try whether folks understand it or not."

"I understand, Grandpa."

Amos stood for a moment and regarded the girl.

"How can you understand something like this, Irma?"

"Because I have dreams. I know that someday I'm going to leave here and do things I've never done before. I'll go whether folks understand it or not."

Amos shook his head and said soberly, "This isn't about following dreams, Irma. You've never made the mistakes I've made. I have to try to right a wrong by bringing Joey back here where he belongs. I wish I could do more, but I can't patch up the problems between your ma and Millie. They're responsible for their own hard feelings toward one another and it will probably take God Almighty to change their minds."

It seemed a strange thing for Amos to say, but it was what he had been feeling lately. He was going to shoulder the responsibilities that were his, do what he could and let his daughters answer for their own sins.

After he had mulled over his reasoning, Amos assured Irma, "I lived in Chicago nearly forty years. I know my way around that town. If they're there, I'll eventually find Millie and Ralph."

"But Grandpa, that's a long trip and you might be gone a long time."

"Don't worry. The Model A will get me to Chicago and back. And you know I know how to get there. I used to drive up here and back for vacation."

"You weren't going alone before, Grandpa."

Amos cast a sly grin in Irma's direction. "I never said I was going alone now. Lloyd is going with me."

"Lloyd!" Irma busted out laughing. "Why are you taking Lloyd?"

"He wants to go and he has a sister there we can stay with. Besides that, he isn't doing anything productive around here. I think Gertie will be happy to get him out of the house for awhile."

"He talks an awful lot, Grandpa."

"Don't worry about that. Lloyd and I will get along just fine."

Irma looked down at the money she held in her hand. "Are you sure you have enough money for yourself? Lloyd doesn't even have enough to pay his bills…"

"He sold his Twin City tractor. He'll be paying his own way and I'll be paying mine. Don't you worry about us. We'll be just fine."

Amos squared his shoulders and moved to the door of Velma's room. He rapped on it.

"Come in," she beckoned softly.

He entered and quickly announced, "Velma, I've come to say good-bye."

She straightened in her rocking chair and looked at her father with a frown. "Good-bye?"

"I'm going to Chicago to get Joey."

Tears brimmed in Velma's eyes. Amos wondered how anyone could cry any more tears than this daughter of his had.

"Oh, Pa, have you heard from Millie? Do you know where she is?" she asked hopefully.

"No, but I think I can find her."

"Where will you go?"

"I know folks in the neighborhood where Ralph lived. I'll start there. It might take a while, but I'm going to find Joey and bring him back, Velma."

"Oh, Pa, thank you. You're doing so much for me."

"I'm not doing it for you, Velma. I'm doing it for me."

Velma looked at him with a puzzled expression. Amos just shook his head. He wouldn't stay and try to explain.

"I've got to get out of here before someone tries to talk some sense into me."

He gave Velma a kiss upon her forehead and gently adjusted the light wrap she had tossed over her shoulders. The thought struck him that all those years of working late at the store had robbed him of the opportunity to tuck his daughters into bed at night. No, he hadn't been robbed. He could have made the opportunity. He just hadn't done it. *I was more concerned about money than I was about how my girls were growing up. Is it too late to remedy any of it?*

Amos spun on his heel and grabbed his bag on the way out the door. *A fool's errand this may be, but I'm nothing but an old fool anyway. I'm going to do what I can to get Joey back or die trying.*

As Amos pulled out of the driveway, he glanced back at the house. Velma was standing at the window, waving at him. Perhaps, he decided, his going had suddenly given her some hope. *Is that what she needed all along? Just a little bit of hope?*

———— ⟳ ————

Amos took a long route to Lloyd's house, reducing his chances of running into John, who was working with the threshing crew a few miles away. As he told Irma, he didn't want anyone reasonable talking him out of doing that which his heart was compelling him to do. Amos was nervous about taking upon himself such a formidable risk, but also had excitement rising within him. He felt almost lighthearted, like a bird released from a cage, and wondered if he had ever been so free before.

When Amos arrived at the Schneider home, Lloyd was sitting on the porch, waiting impatiently. They exchanged greetings as Amos threw his passenger's bag into the back seat. He arranged Lloyd's crutches as best he could while Lloyd cheerily said good-bye to Gertie and climbed into the auto.

Although the two were shirttail kin, Lloyd was opposite Amos in stature and nature. Amos' dark eyes, thick, unruly hair, and burly figure contrasted with Lloyd's slight build, thin hair and light complexion. Where Amos tended to be quiet and contemplative, Lloyd was boisterous and outspoken. Amos knew there would probably be little quiet time on the long journey, but he decided that might be a good thing. If Lloyd was not with him, sense might return and he would stay home, but with Lloyd being excited to visit a sister whom he hadn't seen in years, Amos would not rescind his promise to take the man to Chicago.

"What did John say when you told him you were going to Chicago?" Lloyd asked as soon as the car was out of sight of his house and he was done waving to Gertie.

Amos smiled a wry smile and spoke out of the side of his mouth. "I didn't tell him."

"You asked me not to say anything about it if I saw him and I didn't say a word. I didn't say anything about selling the

Twin City tractor, either. What do you think he'll do when he finds out about that?"

Amos thought about the answer for a while before he spoke. "He'll pitch a fit. But you know, Lloyd, I'm not going to worry about it. John is a grown man. I've got to do what I've got to do and he's got to do what he's got to do. If he's going to be mad, then he's going to be mad. He'll probably get over it by the time I get home."

Lloyd chuckled. "That's right. We've got to mind ourselves and help others when we can, but we can't fix 'em. I'll bet John will stew about how you came up with enough money to go on this trip. He worries about money, I think."

"Yes, he worries. I told him a long time ago I had a bit of cash and I'd help with the bills if need be. He said he didn't need it."

"He's kinda proud that way. Holds on tight to what he's got, doesn't let go of it too easy, and won't admit it when he could use some help."

Kind of like me, Amos thought.

"Does John know how much money you had stashed away, Amos?"

Amos glanced over at Lloyd and grinned, "Nope. He never even asked."

———— ⟨✿⟩ ————

"He did *what*?" John acted as though he hadn't heard Irma right.

"Grandpa left for Chicago this morning. He's going to look for Joey."

"What makes him think he can find Joey? The police can't even find him! We don't even know for sure that Joey is in Chicago!"

"Grandpa used to live there," Irma defended. "He knows where Ralph used to live and work and knows people who know Ralph. He thinks if he can find Ralph, he can find Joey."

"Did you try to talk some sense into him?"

Irma was about to tell her father that Grandpa's decision was a good one and anyone who disagreed with it needed some sense talked into them, but she bit her lip and kept that thought to herself. Her comment was more of a casual one.

"He's been thinking it over for a long time, Pa. His mind is made up."

John wasn't done ranting. "I had a feeling the other day that that old coot was up to something. Whatever made him think he could drive alone all the way to Chicago? He's not as young as he used to be."

Irma planted a devious smile on her face and announced smartly, "He's not alone. Lloyd is with him."

"*Lloyd*? Oh, Lloyd will be a big help! He can't drive the car with that broken leg of his and, he's so fidgety, he'll drive your grandpa to distraction. Furthermore, Lloyd's got no money to pay for *anything*. What was your grandpa thinking?"

Irma giggled at her father's tirade.

"They won't have to pay a lot of money to rent a room," she said. "They're going to stay with Lloyd's sister."

John calmed a bit. "Lloyd's sister. I forgot he had a sister there. At least they'll have somewhere to go, but how can those two afford such a trip?"

"Grandpa dug out the cash money he had saved."

Irma paused and took a deep breath. She didn't intend to be dramatic but she knew her next announcement would be met with more choice words.

"And Lloyd sold the Twin City," she blurted.

"*What*?" John's face blazed crimson and the veins in his neck bulged. Irma recognized the flash of anger in his eyes. "He leaves the country and expects everyone else to help with *his* work and then he sells his tractor that we were going to use to do *his* work!"

John let some uncustomary cuss works escape his lips. A stir behind her alerted Irma that her mother had come from her room. Irma knew the conversation had been overheard.

"What's wrong, John?" Velma asked with genuine concern.

John and Irma glanced at one another. Velma had said so little for so long that her sudden interest in what was bothering others took them both by surprise.

"I'm disgusted with Lloyd and your pa. They're on their way to Chicago, of all stupid things."

"They're going to get Joey."

Velma cast a hopeful smile toward her husband and John quieted. Irma waited, hoping her mother would continue to speak. It had been a long time since her mother had ventured from her room with the deliberate intention of joining into a conversation. Her father, sensing something new in her demeanor, urged Velma to say more.

"You grew up there, Velma. Do you know where Ralph is from?"

"He lived in the Washington Park area and then for a while in Douglas Park."

Those names held no meaning for John. Since milking cows day in and day out didn't lend much time for lengthy travel, he had never had the opportunity to venture as far away as Illinois.

"Do you think your Pa can find Ralph?" he asked.

"It will take him awhile, but Ralph thinks he's a lot smarter than he really is. He has some scheme in mind or he wouldn't have gone back to Chicago. He has dangerous enemies there. He's up to something and it probably has to do with that old gang he ran around with."

Irma glanced once again at her father, who returned her startled look. Not only had her mother become more talkative, but she obviously had been considering her grandfather's difficult mission. And she had just disclosed a more dangerous threat to little Joey than John or Irma had ever imagined.

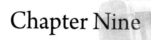

Chapter Nine

For all the energy that Lloyd usually displayed, he was like a little kid in that he couldn't stay awake in a moving automobile. He dozed frequently and snored fitfully. His snorting noises made Amos chuckle. They were a pleasant trade-off for Lloyd's unceasing chatter.

As he drove, Amos contemplated his companion. Lloyd was energetic, but didn't accomplish much in a day compared to a methodical worker like John. Lloyd was kind and helpful, but seemed to be a rather poor manager of money. What troubled Amos was that it didn't bother Lloyd. The man didn't always have a lot, but he was perpetually easy-going and happy and he always seemed to get by. Very seldom did Lloyd seem to have any apprehension or worry.

Amos felt a prick of envy over Lloyd's untroubled nature. Amos had stewed for weeks about spending his hoarded money to go on this trip. Lloyd, being asked two days ago on the spur of the moment, grabbed at the chance with no apparent qualms. Few people could detect when Amos was worried or upset, for he was usually stoic. With Lloyd, everyone knew what he was feeling and why.

Amos recalled the day he went to Millie's empty house where he had been bombarded with devastation and heartache. That day opened his eyes to something he had never admitted to himself before. His family was wretched and troubled. In his heart, perhaps he knew, but he had never faced it until then. He caught himself wondering how differently his daughters might have grown up had they had a father who was more like Lloyd.

The traffic up ahead slowed. Amos let off the gas pedal and downshifted the Model A to allow for the passing of a truck that was hauling dirt. He realized there was a road crew up ahead and, where the repair work was going on, traffic was stopped and waiting.

Since there was a nearby side road that looked like it was unhampered, Amos swung the wheel and aimed his auto down that path. The trail was pleasant and gave Amos a glimpse of country he had never seen before. He enjoyed the peaceful ride, since there was little traffic to contend with.

When the road got bumpy, Lloyd stirred and sat upright.

"Where are we?" he asked as he stretched his arms.

"On a detour. The other road is being worked on."

"Do you know where this one is taking us?"

"We seem to be going around a lake."

"We in Illinois yet?"

"Getting close."

Lloyd stuck his head out the window and gazed at the quiet countryside.

"They seem to be hot and dry like we are up in our neck of the woods," Lloyd said. "But it sure is pretty and there's a lake over there. Do you know what lake it is?"

"I don't know much about the lakes around here."

Lloyd studied his surroundings again.

"There's a car stopped up ahead," he suddenly warned.

"I see that. They must be having trouble."

As they approached, Amos and Lloyd could see two men standing at the side of the road, studying the flat tire on their vehicle. Amos pulled up alongside and Lloyd hollered out the window, "You guys need help?" One of them motioned to them, so Amos pulled over to the side of the road and climbed out of his coupe.

Amos approached the big shiny Buick, thinking that surely these men would have a spare tire and a jack in such a car. As he drew nearer, he realized that both men were far younger and more fit for tire changing than he and Lloyd were. They either didn't know how to do the job or were fearful of getting their fancy business suits soiled. *Or they're trying to entice passersby to stop so they can rob them,* Amos thought with sudden alarm. *It's too late for me to get away. Might as well see how this is going to go.*

"Can I help you fellows?" he asked.

The words nearly caught in his throat when the men turned to him. The shorter of the two smiled and sheepishly admitted their spare tire was not holding air and that they would need a lift to town to get a new tire or repair the old. Amos silently nodded in agreement and pretended that he didn't recognize the hole in the spare tire as one put there by a bullet, as was the hole in the closed trunk lid. He never let on that he figured there were shoulder holsters and guns under those men's suit coats, or that coats were odd things to be wearing while changing tires on a quiet country lane in ninety-five degree weather.

Lloyd hobbled on his crutches toward the men and the thought suddenly struck Amos that Lloyd's mouth might get them into real trouble with this duo.

"We'll go to town and get your tire fixed," Amos hurriedly told the men, "but I don't really know where the nearest town is. I took this road because of the construction on the highway."

"I'll ride with you," the taller man volunteered. "Mr. Hobbs can stay with the car."

The man referred to as Mr. Hobbs nodded in agreement.

As Amos turned toward Lloyd to urge him back into the

Model A, Lloyd blurted, "You want me to stay here and keep you company, Mr. Hobbs? My butt is getting sore from riding."

Mr. Hobbs grinned. "Suit yourself," he replied.

Now you've done it, Lloyd, Amos thought as he helped the taller man lift the damaged tire into his trunk. *I'm leaving you with a gangster. He's got a gun under his coat and probably has enough in the trunk of that car to start a war. You don't have a prayer of getting out of the way if the cops come down this road looking for these guys.*

Amos climbed behind the wheel and, with a slightly trembling hand, set his Model A in motion as soon as his passenger was settled.

"My name is John," the man offered.

"Amos Schultz."

Amos glanced over at him, noting the cleft chin, dark hair and dark eyes. *A nice looking man,* he thought.

"I appreciate you giving us a hand."

His voice was pleasant and calm, but not soothing enough to put Amos at ease.

"I don't like to leave folks stranded."

"Most people would have hit the gas and kept on going when they saw us. If they *had* stopped and gotten out of their auto, they would have run right back to it and taken off."

"My running days are over," Amos assured him.

The man laughed. "I have a feeling you know who I am," he said. "But your friend doesn't know, does he?"

Amos cast another glance at John Dillinger and said, "Believe me, it's better if he doesn't."

———————⌒⌒———————

"Irma tells me Lloyd sold the Twin City tractor. Is that true?"

Gertie smiled excitedly and nodded. "Yes, John."

Inside, John was seething with anger. He addressed his concerns with Gertie through clenched teeth.

"You know Lloyd promised me I could use it for corn cutting and silo filling. If I'm going to help put up your crops, I *need* to use that tractor and I can't pull any felled trees out of the woods to make firewood either. I have to use a tractor or wait until the winter snow so we can use the horses."

"Go right ahead and use the tractor all you want, John. You don't have to ask me."

"When is the new owner coming to pick it up?"

Gertie smiled broadly. "He's already here."

John looked around. The only other person he could see was the hired boy, Allen, who stood a distance away watching the scene.

"John, the tractor is *yours!*" Gertie exclaimed with a gay laugh.

"Mine! I never…"

John suddenly realized where the money for the tractor had come from. "Amos bought it."

"He bought it *for you*. And I have the money Lloyd owed you for fixing it. If you wait here, I'll get it for you. By the way, Lloyd still wants you to take one of the pigs, too."

Gertie was gone for scarcely a minute – long enough for the shocking news to penetrate John's mind. When Gertie handed him the money he was owed, John felt quite sheepish about the reprimands he wanted to level at Lloyd – and Amos.

"That old coot… I could have gotten by with the horses for my own work. He shouldn't have spent his money on this tractor… "

"Or on a trip to Chicago?" Gertie asked the question quietly. She seemed to sense John's misgivings before he voiced them.

"He's wasting his time."

"He's not wasting his time when it's something he has to do. Even if it doesn't work out, he'll feel better knowing he tried.

And Velma will feel better too, knowing that what seemed impossible a while ago might just come to pass. I'm praying that it will."

John ignored Gertie's words about praying for Joey's return. Instead, he admitted aloud that Velma was indeed acting better since her father left.

"I'm glad to hear it, John. I'm anxious to stop in and see her again soon. Now, if you men will put that tractor to work, I've got my own chores to do."

A broad grin softened the stern countenance on John's face. "Yes, ma'am!" he said. He turned to Allen, who waited near the barn for orders. "Let's get this thing to my house. It's time we put it to work!"

Chapter Ten

When her father's truck pulled into the yard, Irma paid little heed – until the Schneider's hired man stepped out from behind the wheel. *Pa let him drive our truck? I don't even get to drive our truck!*

Irma left the clean clothes in the basket with only half of them hung on the line and came across the yard as fast as her short legs would carry her without breaking into a run.

"What are you doing with my pa's truck?" she demanded.

"I brought your pig to ya."

"The pig!"

Irma had forgotten that Lloyd had promised them a pig. She stomped into the cow barn where Phillip was mucking out the gutters. "Do you have a pen ready for the pig yet?" she demanded of her brother.

"We nailed more boards up on the old hog pen behind the shed. It should be ready to go."

"Well, the pig is in a crate in the back of pa's truck, but Pa isn't here to unload it. That kid is here."

Phillip left his task and followed Irma outside. To Irma's consternation, Shirley had come from the house and was greeting Allen as though they were the best of friends. While they conversed, Phillip set to work putting up some tattered gates that would hopefully guide the pig into its new home.

Irma tromped away toward the clothesline. She was still seething with anger that her father would entrust his truck to that ornery orphan kid. *And where has Pa gone off to? He had to have gone to the Schneiders. That means he's probably driving the tractor home.*

Irma was securing a kitchen towel on the line when there was an awful crash. Shirley screamed, the boys hollered, the pig squealed and suddenly they were all streaking toward her. She dove from behind her freshly hung laundry in time to thwart the speeding creature from coming near it. The pig turned and the boys followed, running as fast as they could – right toward the garden.

"Don't you dare wreck that garden!" Irma screamed.

She took off after the wayward animal, racing past the porch as her mother came outside to investigate the ruckus. Shirley grabbed a hoe that was resting upon the side of the house and took off after the wayward half-grown swine, wielding the hoe as a weapon. Once the animal was safely out of the garden, Irma stopped her pursuit. The others fanned out, taking turns trailing the pig which led them across the edge of the field. It took awhile, but the trio of pursuers eventually got the animal headed back toward the buildings.

Irma went to the granary and half-filled a bucket with newly threshed oats. "Suey!" she called. She dribbled the grain on the ground, hoping to entice the animal to stop and eat. The first couple laps around the place, the pig showed no desire to stop for anything. But after several minutes of running past one pursuer to be accosted by another, the animal's stamina waned. It finally decided to check out the tasty morsels at Irma's feet.

Moments later, the little hog went from eating sparse grains off the ground to gobbling mouthfuls from the proffered bucket. And the animal scarcely noticed that, as it ate, Irma was backing it around the barn toward its pen. As soon as it was in the confines of the boarded up pen, Irma tossed the rest of the grain and grabbed for the gate to shut it. She was just getting it secured when the others arrived, out of breath from their merry chase.

"That's how you get a pig to go where you want it to go," she said smartly. "Stick their head in a bucket and back them up. Saves chasing them around all day."

Her words were mostly directed at that hired kid. Irma wondered why Lloyd and Gertie would put up with such an incompetent farmer's helper. He obviously didn't know anything about farm animals!

A bump at the back of Irma's legs told her that the gate was not secure enough for it budged. The pig hit it a second time and before she or anyone else could make the loose board fast, the determined pig slammed into it and was on the way out!

"No, you don't!" Irma cried. She grabbed the animal. The boys closed in, ready to come to Irma's aid. The pig panicked and squirmed. Before Irma could steady herself, she was pushed backwards, lost her balance and landed on her backside in a pile of manure that Phillip had just removed from the barn.

"You stupid pig!" she screamed as she scrambled up out of the mess.

"Looks like pigs can shove *people* backwards, too!" Allen taunted.

He started to laugh at her, but his howls were short-lived. Irma scooped up a handful of the barnyard mess and fired it at him. Much to her surprise, it hit him fully in the face with a splat.

He spit, he sputtered and then he came after her. When he reached for her, she kicked him in the knee with her bare foot, which instantly hurt like the dickens. He winced. She made ready to do more damage if he came any closer.

As Allen stepped near enough to shove her back into the manure, Irma let out a bellow and dove at him in an attempt to unbalance him. Her intent was to throw him into the same smelly pile.

They were both suddenly grabbed around their necks by a pair of firm hands.

"That's enough!" John bellowed.

All thoughts of fighting were immediately dispelled.

"Phillip, you and Allen go to the creek and wash up. Don't come back to the house until I call for you. Irma, you go behind the lilac bushes and take off those filthy clothes!"

Phillip asked, "What about the pig, pa?"

"We'll catch it when everyone has calmed down. Now go do as I said!"

Irma marched out of the barnyard without a backward glance at her enemy. The oozing, smelly muck clung to her back, dripped from her hair, and stuck between her toes, but she was so steaming mad she scarcely noticed.

Behind her, she could hear her father instructing Shirley to fetch her sister some clean clothes and put some water on the stove to boil while he hauled the washtub outside. Shirley giggled and Irma whirled around, ready to give her a tongue-lashing. Much to her chagrin, her father wasn't keeping a straight face either.

Irma was truly astounded when she fled around the corner of the house and found her mother sitting on the steps, doubled over and laughing hysterically.

Lloyd stuck his head out the window and waved vigorously as Amos started his Model A and put it into gear. As they drove away from the newly repaired Buick, Lloyd settled back into his seat with a pleased smile on his face.

"That Mr. Hobbs is a real nice guy," he declared. "He really likes kids and told me about his kids. He was really sorry to hear about Joey being taken away from his mama. That's why he was asking those questions about Ralph. I told him about Ralph maybe being a con man and that there were three or four stores that got robbed up north while Ralph lived there and they even found money missing from the place where he used to work."

Amos groaned inwardly. He could only wonder how much information Mr. Hobbs had learned in the time it took to buy a new tire and put it on the car.

Amos was tempted to explain to Lloyd that if Amos had tried anything foolish, like telling the tire salesman he was picking up a tire for John Dillinger, Lloyd would have suffered for it. Lloyd was essentially held hostage and didn't even know it. He was enjoying his visit with Mr. Hobbs!

"Wouldn't that be something if those men found Joey for you?" Lloyd chattered. "It's well worth it to stop and help folks. They might be able to help you in return and they even paid you for your trouble!"

Amos appreciated the money he was given, but snickered at the notion of getting any help from the likes of those men.

"I doubt they'll have time to look for Joey. They've got better things to do. Besides, they didn't say they were going to Chicago, did they?"

"Not that I recall. And Mr. Hobbs never told me exactly what they did for a living, but I think they must be salesmen or bankers or something."

Amos almost busted out laughing. He had to turn his face from Lloyd for a moment so Lloyd wouldn't detect his merriment. *What would Lloyd do if I told him who those men were?*

"I gave Mr. Hobbs my sister's address and phone number, just in case."

"In case of what?" Amos asked. He had let his mind wander and became alarmed when Lloyd said what he did.

"In case those men find Joey. They need to know where to bring him, don't they?"

Amos bit back a scathing criticism of how foolish and naïve Lloyd was. He commanded himself to settle down. *Don't worry.*

Dillinger and Hobbs have already forgotten about us. They aren't looking for Joey and they won't be calling on us at Lloyd's sister's house. Our association with them is over and done. I hope.

---◌◞◟◌---

"I don't understand why those two hate each other. I don't think they've ever once said a kind word to one another."

John whispered it to Velma as she lay the sleeping baby in her cradle and readied herself for bed. For weeks, he had been sleeping outside under the stars, for it was cooler outside than inside. The truth was that he had been so uncomfortable with Velma's sorry state that trying to rest on the hard ground was the easier option. Now, since Velma was improving, he ventured to take his rightful place beside his wife. It felt pretty good to lie down on his own bed again.

"Irma is jealous," Velma explained.

"Jealous of what?"

"You let Allen drive your truck. Irma never gets to drive your truck."

"Are you sure?"

"I asked her why she disliked Allen. She said she doesn't like the way he acts. He stares at her and argues with her and she doesn't like it that he got to drive your truck."

"I don't let her drive my truck because I never taught her how to drive it. I never taught her how to drive it because I didn't think she could see over the steering wheel."

Velma giggled. The sound was pleasant in John's ears.

"She's not much shorter than I am. I think I could drive your truck, if you taught me how. You should at least let her try."

"She'd better practice with the automobile first. Maybe we should let Irma take it to Gertie's house. She needs as much practice making doughnuts as she does driving."

"You just want doughnuts."

John snickered and didn't deny it.

Velma suggested, "If we send her over to the Schneider's, she might have another run in with Allen. We should probably keep those two separated as much as possible."

"Maybe we should let them fight it out and be done with it."

John ceased talking about his daughter. He looked quietly at his wife as she moved about the room in the dim light and recalled the first time he had ever seen this dark-eyed beauty. She was sitting in the back seat of her father's 1914 Model T Ford. John hadn't learned her name on that first encounter, but wished he had. Before she left Brill, he had gotten her name and address as well. By the time she returned the following year, they had written countless letters to one another and the next time she made the trip from Chicago, she came to him as a bride.

"What are you thinking?" she asked as she slipped into bed beside him.

John reached out to caress her soft cheek. "Thinking about all those letters we wrote to one another. I waited a long time for you."

"I told you I loved you."

"And I said the same."

"I still do, John Connor. I still love you."

John hugged her close. She returned his embrace and then reached up and traced the contour of his forehead, nose, and lips. In that tender moment, John felt as though she was trying to assure him everything would be all right – that she would be all right. For a while, they both put their worries behind them.

Chapter Eleven

Amos waited impatiently to buy the postage he needed to mail a letter to Velma. He wasn't much at writing letters, but had penned a short note to let his daughter know he had made it safely to Chicago and was settled into a room in Lloyd's sister's house. He didn't mention any incidents along the way.

Amos had a feeling that Lloyd would not sit patiently outside and, sure enough, before he got to the post office window to get his stamps, Lloyd entered. Amos expelled some pent up air as he turned to the teller to finish his business. He hoped Lloyd would find someone to talk to and that he would keep his eyes off the posters on the wall.

As soon as the letter was mailed, Amos turned to go. *Too late!* Lloyd was standing at the wall, studying the wanted posters and growing paler by the second. When Amos approached, Lloyd turned to him and began stammering. Amos hurried him out the door as fast as he could shove a crippled man without sending them both tumbling into the street.

"A…Amos, did you see…?"

Amos motioned him to stay quiet.

"But, Amos, that was John Di…Dill…"

Amos clasped a hand over Lloyd's mouth and snarled, "Shut up, Lloyd!"

One of the patrons came out into the street and asked, "Is something wrong?"

"He's having one of his spells," Amos shouted over Lloyd's protests. "I've got to get him home… to get his medicine…"

"But, Amos..."

"For once in your life, shut your mouth!" Amos hissed.

He shoved Lloyd through the open door of the automobile. As soon as Lloyd and his confounded crutches were stuffed into the cab, Amos slammed the door shut and spat through the open window, "Keep your mouth shut until we get out of here!"

Lloyd was clearly taken aback by Amos' menacing words. He sat in his seat with a stricken look on his face. Sweat beaded on his brow and his lips moved, but he remained silent until Amos got settled in the vehicle and started it.

"Amos, that man we helped – that was John Dillinger!"

"I know."

"What you mean, you know?"

"Just what I said!"

"Why didn't you tell me?"

"Because I was afraid you'd have a heart attack and I didn't want to deal with you having a heart attack!"

"I'm not going to have a heart attack. But... we can't just drive away and not tell anybody. We should tell the police we saw Dillinger!"

Amos leveled an imposing glance at Lloyd and argued, "We're not telling *anybody* we saw Dillinger. He and Mr. Hobbs said they'd help us find Joey and we're not ratting on them."

Lloyd sat in sullen silence for a few moments and then blurted out, "That's why you didn't want me in the post office! You didn't want me to see Dillinger's wanted poster! You knew who it was we were helping."

"I read a newspaper every now and then, Lloyd. Once in a while they put pictures in a newspaper."

"Well, we shouldn't have helped them."

"What was I supposed to do, Lloyd? You were outside of the car, standing there with one gangster and I was inside the car with the other one. Any shenanigans and we'd have ended up *dead*."

As Amos navigated the busy streets, Lloyd contemplated the situation with furrowed brow. When he spoke, it was in an apologetic manner.

"I don't think they'll help you find Joey, Amos. They were just being nice, being you got that tire for them. They're so busy... you know, robbing banks and police stations and the like... they don't have time to help folks like us look for a missing boy."

"You're right, but we're *still* not going to tell anyone we saw them. We're not taking the chance on getting into trouble with those two."

"They got no reason to give us trouble."

"If we told the police where we saw them, you think they wouldn't guess who told? We'd have big trouble!"

"They don't know where to find us..."

Lloyd's face suddenly turned white as a sheet. Amos knew that Lloyd realized his mistake, but he reiterated Lloyd's thoughts anyway and did it with a sly grin.

"That's right, Lloyd. You gave them your sister's address, just in case they find Joey."

Amos thought for a moment that Lloyd was going to pass out. He chuckled.

"Amos?" Lloyd asked with a slight quiver in his voice.

"What, Lloyd?"

"Do you know who Mr. Hobbs is?"

Amos glanced over at his passenger.

"You can tell me, Amos. I promise I won't have a heart attack."

"I don't know."

"Are you just saying that?"

"No! I don't know who Mr. Hobbs really is and I don't want to know."

"Do you know if Mr. Hobbs is his real name?"

"I don't know. I don't want to know."

Lloyd sat in silence for quite some time and then suddenly laughed aloud before saying, "I can't wait to tell Gertie."

Chapter Twelve

"Why are you limping, Irma?"

Irma was making tea for her mother and their guest and pretended she didn't hear Mrs. Schneider's question. *I'm not going to tell her my foot hurts because I kicked her hired man in the leg.*

"Irma's foot has been bothering her since that day Allen delivered the pig," Velma told Gertie. "Did Allen tell you about the trouble we had?"

"He didn't say much, but he did tell me there was a problem when I asked why he got home so late."

The problem started, Irma thought to herself, *because Allen was paying more attention to Shirley than he was to helping Phillip get the pig out of the crate and into the pen.*

"Allen didn't mention a spat with Irma?"

Irma had hoped her mother would turn the conversation elsewhere instead of fanning the flames. She could feel a flush of embarrassment creeping into her cheeks.

"He didn't say a thing about it. But I would like to know what happened, if you'll tell me."

Gertie's statement was directed at Irma, but Irma could see that her mother was anxious to tell the tale so she remained silent.

"The pig pushed Irma backward and she landed in the manure. When Allen laughed at her, she threw some of it at him. John got home in time to stop the battle before they started throwing punches, but not before Irma kicked Allen in the leg."

Gertie didn't take the news of the altercation too well. She did not make excuses for Allen, nor did she threaten to reprimand him. She quietly contemplated the news until Dorothy let out a wail. Out of habit, Irma moved to get her out of her cradle. Velma held up her hand, indicating that Irma should stay in the kitchen and leave the baby's care to her. When she left the room, Gertie addressed Irma.

"Will *you* tell me what happened?"

"You heard all you need to," Irma said. "I fell in the manure and Allen laughed at me. I got mad and flung some in his face…"

"In his face?"

"A handful of it."

"Oh, Irma!"

"Pa made him and Phillip go down to the stream and wash up while I was taking a bath by the house. That's why Allen was so late getting back to your place."

"You got that mad because he laughed at you?"

"He thought it was funny because the pig pushed me backwards. I pushed the pig backwards to get it into the pen and… I was talking pretty smart about it since no one else could catch the thing."

"Why were you talking smart about it?"

Irma well knew Mrs. Schneider's habit of posing questions in order to get people to see things in a different light. But Irma wasn't ready to admit to wrongdoing on her part, so she answered the question with an arrogant air.

"Because I know more about handling pigs than he does."

"Why is it important to you to show him how much smarter you are than he is? Is it so hard to help others learn something new? Or is it something about Allen that bothers you?"

Each question seemed to be more penetrating than the last one. Irma didn't have a good answer for any of them so she remained silent.

"You don't respect him as a person," Mrs. Schneider gently

admonished. "Is it because he came from the orphanage? He can't help what's happened in his life."

"That has nothing to do with it! I'll respect him when he respects me! The first time he ever saw me, he accused me of being twelve and he said he wasn't taking any orders from me."

"And you *politely* corrected him?"

Irma paused again. What was it she had said to him? Whatever it was, she knew it wasn't polite.

"I guess I told him I was older than he was," Irma confessed. "Then we got in a fight about how old we were."

"And then?"

"Then he went and sat down on the chopping block and started eating doughnuts, right in front of me, teasing me with them."

Gertie laughed aloud. She was still laughing when Velma returned to the room with Dottie cradled in her arms.

"I don't know how to make Irma and Allen be civil to one another," Gertie told Velma with a chuckle. "I'll just have to talk to God about it and hope He sees fit to change a couple people's attitudes."

Gertie turned her attention to Velma and commented, "You're looking better every time I see you, Velma."

Irma was glad the conversation had steered away from her and Allen, but she wasn't prepared for her mother's quiet remark.

"I have Irma to thank for a lot of my healing." Velma hesitated, then shyly confessed to her daughter, "I overheard you that Sunday morning when you announced to everyone that you were not going to let your dreams and faith die. I was feeling sorry for myself. I didn't think I could go on with so much worry and hurt. Then I heard my little girl and she was being so brave. It still took me awhile to push myself out of my weeping chair, but I finally started thinking about my family again and not so much about myself. Then, when Pa left..."

Velma stopped speaking. Tears clouded her eyes.

"Your father is doing so much to try to help you," Gertie offered by way of comfort.

Velma shook her head. "He's not doing it for me. He told me he's doing it for himself. He didn't explain what he meant, but I think I know. It's not like my father to spend his hard-earned money on something from which there may be no return. He has always been so concerned with money and controlled every bit of ours. He provided very well for my mother and Millie and me, but I think we had a nice house and nice clothes so Amos Schultz could say he was prosperous. In his heart, he has not been a giving person – until now. Something is changing him."

Irma suddenly recalled the conversation she had been having with God when Allen appeared. She had been contemplating God's refining process and had asked God to polish her. Polishing meant taking the rough edges off of something. Maybe Grandpa had asked God to change him, too.

"Maybe he's getting refined, like the pastor talked about," Irma quietly suggested.

"What do you mean?" Velma asked.

"Irma is referring to the sermon from a few weeks ago," Gertie said. "The pastor explained how gold and silver are tried and how God can use troubles to make people kinder, stronger or more obedient to His Word."

At Velma's request, Gertie launched into a more detailed explanation of the sermon. Irma turned her thoughts back to the polishing she had asked God to do. *Maybe God's idea of polishing me was to send someone who rubbed me the wrong way like Allen does. If so, I don't like it one bit.*

———— ⌒ ————

"John, will you come to church with us?"

Velma was fixing her hair and had donned an old dress that hadn't been out of the closet in some time, for she had long ago deemed it unfashionable. That she would wear it to church signaled to John that she was serious about going and that her intent was not to impress anyone.

"You know, I have always liked that dress on you," he said.

The dress did look nice on her, but John was using the complement to subvert Velma's plot to drag him to church. He was stalling for time in hope that she and the girls would leave without him.

Velma blushed. She was flattered, but made a simple excuse for its disuse. "I always thought I'd remake it for one of the girls. I never got around to it."

"I'm glad you didn't."

He caressed her back and watched her put the finishing touches on her wavy hair.

She turned to him and asked again, "Won't you come with us, John?"

A line of worry creased Velma's brow. Pain and uncertainty clouded her eyes.

How can I refuse such a simple request? After all these weeks, she's finally ready to get out of the house. I shouldn't hold her back. If I don't go, will she change her mind?

John relented. It had been months since he'd darkened the doors of the church. He hadn't wanted to go, since churches always seemed to have a need for money. John had none to give and he didn't want to hear any begging. People everywhere were in desperate circumstances and he, like they, needed every penny to keep their families off the poor farm. He was helping others the best he could and even that was leaving him feeling as though he was stretched too thin.

I used to enjoy going to church, but my heart is not in this anymore. What's happened to me?

"Velma, it is so good to see that you're getting out and about again."

The greeting came from one of the neighbor women. Another turned her attention to Irma, who was holding the baby.

"Look at little Dottie! She is getting cuter every week, isn't she?"

Several women gathered round to greet Velma and Irma. When Gertie tickled Dorothy under the chin, the babe smiled and cooed.

Irma shifted the baby in her arms and said, "She's getting heavier every day!"

"I'll take her, Irma," her mother offered. "You'd best go visit with the young folks."

Irma handed Dottie off to her mother, a bit worried as to whether her mother had the strength to stand and hold such a wiggly little one for long, but then realized there were plenty of other eager arms that would coddle Dottie.

As Irma strode away from the women, she noted that her father was in deep conversation with some farmers with whom he had been working. She was pleasantly surprised when she walked past the men to discover that they were talking about baseball instead of poor cattle prices. *I'm glad for that. Pa needs to relax instead of thinking about work all the time.*

Irma neared a group of young people and immediately saw that Allen was standing close to the very people she wished to speak with. *He's not chasing me away from my friends!* she vowed. She strode toward them and greeted the group with a cheery smile on her lips. She ignored Allen.

"How are you doing, Irma?" one asked. "I didn't get to talk to you the past couple of weeks since everyone was crowding around to look at the baby."

"I got to hold Dottie last week," another said. "She sure is cute and she never makes a fuss. I sure wish the kids I mind every day were so good."

Irma resented all the talk about her baby sister. She would have liked to talk about dresses or nice looking boys or something. If Allen hadn't been standing within earshot, she would have told her friends how insolent he was and how she got back at him when he tried to make a fool of her.

She glanced his way and found to her horror that he was staring at her with his searching nut-brown eyes. She cast a scowl in his direction and turned away, but couldn't help overhearing what he said to a couple guys next to him.

"You'd think nobody around here ever saw a baby before, the way they make such a to-do about hers."

The remark pierced Irma to the core. She clenched her fists. *That no good, dirty rotten scum! Does he think Dottie is my baby?*

Laughter behind her caused Irma to swirl around and face her enemy. Allen was being laughed at by Shirley, who had also heard the comment. Shirley promptly set him straight.

"Dottie isn't Irma's baby. She's our baby sister!"

A sheepish look passed over Allen's face, but he said nothing by way of apologizing for his blunder. Shirley, in her young innocence, didn't seem to realize the implications of Allen's attitude toward someone he thought was a young unwed mother. She turned the conversation back to a new job she was starting, while Irma stood in silent, seething anger.

What kind of girl does he think I am? She wanted to demand an answer from Allen, but was not going to do it in front of her acquaintances or the church crowd. As long as he was helping her father and brothers with work, Irma knew she would have an opportunity to have it out with him. And boy, was she going to take it.

Chapter Thirteen

Her pa's Model A pickup truck lurched when Irma pulled her foot off the clutch. She was glad her pa wasn't there to watch her bumpy progress down the drive. He would be shouting instructions and making her more nervous than she already was. Chickens scattered in every direction, leaving off their pecking for grit and bugs along the driveway to escape the unpredictable path of the jerking vehicle bearing down upon them.

Pa had never properly taught Irma how to operate the vehicle, but she had had a little practice with the automobile. It had taken awhile to start the truck, but she figured out how to turn on the fuel and push the button on the floor to start the engine. Once she figured out how to shift, she was on her way.

Irma's plans were to enjoy the beautiful fall day by digging some of the root vegetables that remained in the garden. Her intentions had not involved taking her father's truck – not until Mrs. Schneider came by to pick up her mother for an apple peeling. An apple peeling meant some delicious apple butter would soon be in the making. Irma's mouth watered just thinking about it.

When she came, Mrs. Schneider brought a message for Phillip to take the truck and spare parts for the corn binder to the field. Phillip was to stop at the Schneider's and pick up Allen on the way and then get to the field as soon as he could. But Irma's father had forgotten Phillip was to help on another farm that day and was already gone.

He's only fourteen and not much taller than me, Irma reasoned. *Pa lets him drive the truck and he let Harvey drive it a couple times, too. He's only eleven! And Harvey's out herding cattle. I'm the only one left who can take the parts to Pa.*

Even if they had a telephone, there was no way Irma could reach her father to tell him of the predicament. She would have to handle things herself. Irma had quickly tossed all manner of machine parts into the box of the truck, not knowing which ones her father needed. She knew her driving skills were sorely lacking, but she was determined and figured she would be a proficient driver by the time she got to the Schneider's house. She didn't relish picking up Allen to take him to where her pa was working, but if that was the price for her chance to drive, so be it.

Thankfully, the road to the Schneider's house was sparsely traveled in the middle of the morning. Irma practiced changing gears while aiming the vehicle in a straight path and had them figured out to where she hardly ground them at all by the time she reached her destination.

When she pulled into the yard, she was immediately met with a glare from Allen, who came from Lloyd's shed with some tools in a bucket. He obviously was expecting a ride and was sorely disappointed to see who was giving it.

Now is my chance to have it out with him, Irma told herself. She immediately began rethinking her intentions. *I don't feel like being refined the hard way, Lord. Maybe Allen and I can quietly discuss our misunderstandings.*

Irma looked at Allen, searching for the right thing to say and finding that saying something civil to him was harder than she realized. He stared back at her and said nothing, just chewed the side of his lip. She hadn't noticed that he had that habit until now.

"Are we going to stare at one another all day or are you going to get in so I can take you to work?"

"I don't want you driving me to work. You ain't no good at driving that truck."

Irma's temper started to simmer. She took a deep breath to calm herself and said, "Ma says I need the practice. Pa wouldn't let me drive it because he didn't think I could reach the pedals and see over the hood, but I can. I drove all the way over here without any problems."

"It didn't sound to me like you weren't having problems. I heard you coming from two miles down the road."

"I was practicing shifting."

Allen didn't get into the truck.

"I've got to get going. The men are waiting for parts. Do you want me to tell them you aren't going to help them?"

"If I don't want to help with something, I'll tell them myself. I ain't leaving it for you to do."

Irma didn't forfeit her driver's seat, so Allen lifted the bucket of tools into the back of the pickup box and then hopped in and settled down among the array of metal parts.

"Get going!" he hollered.

"Suit yourself," Irma mumbled.

She started the engine and attempted to get the transmission into reverse so she could turn the truck around. She had never tried that gear before and the truck protested with an agitated grinding when she pushed on the lever.

"Push the clutch in farther!"

Irma bit back a sharp retort. She shifted her position forward on the seat and shoved the clutch down as best she could. The lever slipped into position and the grinding stopped. She eased her foot off the clutch and shoved the gas pedal with the other. The truck jerked and then sailed backwards at an alarming speed. Irma punched the brake pedal. Metal parts shifted position in the back of the truck and Allen let out a string of cuss words. Irma became more nervous, but also more determined to show him she could conquer the driving task.

She put the truck into first gear, turned the wheel to direct the vehicle from the edge of a weed patch to the drive and then eased the clutch slowly. She pushed the gas pedal more gently than before and the truck only lurched a little as she drove forward.

Thump! The sudden lift and drop of the rear wheel surprised Irma. The truck halted. She tried again to ease it forward, but it wouldn't go. She put it into reverse and gave it more gas. The tires spun but didn't move the truck a bit.

Irma looked back, knowing Allen would probably have something to say about her predicament, but he was looking over the side of the box and shaking his head. She dove out of the cab to see what could have been hiding in the overgrown foliage into which she had driven. A light drag was laying there. She had run over the corner of it with the back tire and the tire sunk into the space between two of the bars.

"I didn't see that there! Do you think I can get it out without ruining the tire?"

Allen eased his lanky frame from out of the back of the truck and squatted down to survey the situation more closely.

"You can't see over the hood. You can't see what's behind you. You shouldn't be driving."

"I just need practice and you could have told me there was machinery laying there. I would have turned the front wheels the other way and missed it."

"Girls shouldn't be driving trucks."

That did it. Irma was done being nice for the day.

"Why do you hate me so much? What's the reason for it?" The challenge flew out of her mouth. "You hated me even before I threw that manure at you. You've been spiteful ever since you first saw me and I want to know why!"

"You weren't nice to me. You thought I was a begging bum."
He didn't yell the words, for which Irma felt a tinge of relief.

"Yes, I thought you were a bum and I wasn't nice to you, but you didn't think the best of me either."

Allen chewed on the side of his mouth. He knew to what false notions she was referring and seemed to be pondering what to say about the situation.

"Let's just drop it," Irma suggested. "We started out with wrong ideas about each other and now we're just accusing each other and not apologizing. We're not getting anywhere and I've got to get these parts to the field."

Irma tromped back toward the cab and climbed into the seat.

"What do you think you're going to do?"

"Try again to back the truck out of the hole I got it in."

"You'll probably ruin the tire, like you said."

"I don't know what else to do but try."

Allen stood by and watched as she attempted to back the truck out of its predicament. The tires spun and spit dirt that flew past the cab, but the back wheel remained firmly lodged. Irma flung the door open and stormed out of the cab once again.

"What do you think you're going to do now?" Allen asked with a tinge of a smart-alecky smile on his lips.

"I'm going to get the jack out, jack up the back of the truck, and put something under the tire."

Irma dug under the truck seat and pulled at the jack her father kept there. The thing wouldn't budge. When she investigated the problem, she found that her father had made a narrow box to keep the jack, the handle, and a few odd tools snug in their places. The toolbox was bolted down and Irma couldn't get the nut loosened.

"Can I borrow a wrench?" she asked Allen.

"What size?"

"About this big," she said as she held up her thumb and forefinger, indicating the width of the square nut.

Allen shook his head and fetched three wrenches out of the bucket. Instead of offering any to her, he squeezed into the narrow space, forcing Irma to back up, and tackled the problem himself.

Once the jack was free, he set it under the rear axle and expertly screwed the jack, lifting the back of the truck inch by inch until the tire cleared the side rail of the drag.

"I think we can move the drag out of the way easier than trying to wedge something under the tire," he suggested.

Irma eyed the array of burning nettles and burdocks surrounding the drag and resigned herself to the painful job of trying to move it. She tromped down the weeds as best she could, clearing a path to one side of the drag while Allen headed for the other end. They lifted opposite corners of the implement, which came up off the ground easier than Irma thought it would. It had been used just a few months ago, so it was not embedded in the soil, but ensnarled in the weeds. It didn't have to be moved far to clear the tire, just a few inches.

Irma jerked at the thing with all her might, which loosed it from under the truck tire, but also twisted the ungainly piece of equipment. It sprang back at her when Allen heaved on his end. The weight of the section that Irma was holding tipped her backward. She lost her balance and dropped her end as she plopped into a pile of weeds. The sudden shift and jerking of the drag sent Allen spilling headlong into his own end of the weed patch.

Allen was the first to clamor out of the mess. Irma was a bit slower getting up and was truly surprised when he asked if she was okay.

"That hurt!" Irma complained. "I landed in the nettles and that thing landed on my foot."

"So you have a sore foot again?" he teased.

She smiled. "At least this time I didn't kick anybody to get it."

The two emerged from opposite ends of the weed patch with late-summer burdocks stuck to them in abundance.

"I look like I've been in a burr fight," Irma muttered as she came around the truck, busily ridding herself of the offending stickers.

Allen laughed at her. When she glanced up at him, she, too, busted out laughing.

"You have a ball of burs on top of your head!" she shrieked.

He ducked down to review the mess in the truck's side mirror and touched the odd adornment as though it were a fashionable top hat. With a grin, he turned to Irma and said, "You have them in your hair and all over your dress."

Irma didn't need to look in the mirror to survey her situation. She could feel the pricks of burrs all up and down her back and there were wads of them like tufts on her skirt. Her hair was pulled by the stickers into an odd knot at the side of her head.

"I guess I won't be driving the truck out to the field," she admitted with a giggle. "I can't get into the truck cab without getting burrs stuck all over the seat."

Allen looked at her with a mischievous grin and admitted, "I don't think I'll be driving either. Not until I get the stickers off of me."

He turned around and displayed a fine array of weedy decorations stuck to his back.

"We better get at cleaning ourselves up," Irma said.

They plucked at the offending, itching pricklers, tossing aside handfuls of the stuff. Irma suddenly felt very awkward doing it. She knew they both needed the help of the other to rid themselves of the burrs. Allen knew it too and time was wasting. There were machine parts needed in the field.

"I'll pull the burrs off your back so you can drive," she offered.

Allen nodded in agreement. "It will be easier than getting you cleaned up."

He turned his back to her and she began the plucking process. As soon as she was finished, he turned to her.

"I'll get them off you, too."

Irma felt a moment of alarm. Allen had been her enemy such a short time ago. Now, he was being civil. Dare she trust him to help her? Or was he scheming a way of revenge?

"You'd better go deliver the parts. I'll stay here and pick burrs."

"Are you sure?"

Irma nodded. She knew it was the best option. "I'll clean up and then walk home."

"Okay." Allen moved to the truck and opened the door. "Are you all right?" he asked.

Irma nodded again. For some strange reason, tears misted her eyes for a moment, and it wasn't because her arm itched and the burdocks pricked. Allen was being kind and his sudden change in demeanor touched her unexpectedly.

He started the engine and Irma suddenly came alert.

"Hey!" she shouted above the roar of the engine. "Let down the jack!"

Allen climbed sheepishly out of the cab and did as he was bidden. When the jack and handle were returned to their place under the seat, he turned to Irma, looked at her with that penetrating stare, then leaned down and planted a kiss upon her lips. She didn't protest, didn't argue, just wondered at the quickening sensation in her heart. When Allen moved to kiss her again, she let him do so.

"I think I liked it better when you two were fighting like cats and dogs!"

Irma shoved Allen away from her and looked around in horror to see how her father had approached them without being heard. With no vehicle about, it was obvious he had walked across the fields to investigate the delay in getting his parts. Now, he had found Irma in Allen's arms, looking like a sorry mess and completely forgetting about the machinery that needed repair.

"Get in the truck!"

"Pa, I'm full of burrs. I can't sit down on the seat. I was going to stay here and pick burrs off of me and Allen was going to take the parts to you."

"Allen, get in the truck."

John climbed into the cab. Allen slipped quietly into the passenger seat. He didn't turn around to look at her, but as they sped out of the Schneider's driveway, Irma caught the slight wave Allen offered as he hung his hand out the open window. Irma's foot throbbed, her arms stung, and her back itched like crazy, but she felt as though her heart was singing.

———————⟡———————

"I got a letter from father," Velma said. "He didn't say much, just told me that he and Lloyd arrived in Chicago safely and Lloyd's sister was thrilled to see him. She'll put them up as long as they want to stay, since they are paying her and she needs help with her bills."

"That's a relief." John's response was automatic and insincere, for his mind was not on Amos' jaunt to Chicago.

"Is there something wrong?" Velma asked.

"Guess who kissed Irma today?"

"What?"

"You heard me."

"She was supposed to pick up Allen…"

"And she got the truck stuck in the Schneider's yard. By the time they got it out, they had not only made a truce, but when I walked into the yard, they were kissing."

Velma giggled. "Gertie said she was going to pray that they would have a change of attitude."

"I wish Gertie would have kept her nose out of it! They've had a change of attitude, all right. I liked it better when they were fighting."

"Irma was bound to get a kiss sooner or later."

"It should be later."

"She'll be seventeen in a few days."

John let out a long sigh. "Seventeen. Our kids are growing up. They'll be leaving home before we know it."

"We've got to let them all go someday. Maybe I'll be ready when the time comes. I'm getting a change of attitude."

"Gertie praying for you, too?"

"For all of us, I'm sure. And when Gertie was here the other day, I found out that Irma was praying that God would refine her."

"What do you mean by that?"

"You know, take off the rough edges and make her more Christ-like. Apparently the pastor had a sermon about it a few weeks ago – something about God being like a refiner of silver or gold."

John settled down on the bed with his hands behind his head and thought about what Velma said. He knew a thing or two about metals. It took the right amount of heat and patience to purge impurities from gold and silver. He could well imagine the kind of sermon that the preacher had made of it. It was sure to be something about trials doing someone good. John wondered if, years down the road, his family would say that the lean years had somehow made them better people.

When Velma slipped into bed beside him, John said quietly, "I suppose it's not a bad prayer. We all need refining, don't we?"

In the dim light, John saw that Velma cast him a smile as she said, "Yes, John, we do."

Chapter Fourteen

Amos parked his car on a side street and quietly watched the passersby. He had waited on one street after another for weeks, patiently watching the activity in each neighborhood and hoping for a glimpse of Ralph or Millie.

What if I'm wrong? What if they moved to Detroit or St. Paul instead of coming back to Chicago?

Doubts nagged at him daily, but Amos persisted in his conviction that Ralph was here. *Ralph has contacts and allies here. He wouldn't go anywhere else.*

Amos had been making discreet inquiries and was ever hopeful that someone would give him a lead. A few people had seen someone of Millie's description and the woman had a little curly-haired boy with her. *She's here somewhere. I know it.*

"Beatrice?" He whispered his wife's name as though she were sitting next to him. "We didn't do right by Millie. That girl was spoiled rotten and..."

The passenger door popped open and Amos suddenly found a companion in his car.

"You lookin' for Ralph Castellani?" the man asked as he pulled the door shut.

"Yes."

"Follow that black car up ahead."

Amos did as he was told and stayed close behind the bumper of a sleek sedan.

"He's been casin' out stores over in Washington Park. He's got the lady and kid with him."

"He's robbing stores and has Millie and Joey helping him do it?"

Amos' heart sank as quickly as when he first realized Millie was gone with the boy.

"The lady goes in, the kid distracts the shopkeeper and Ralphy grabs something off the shelves or dips outta the till. Small jobs, ya know? But a couple times he and a buddy pulled guns and demanded money. Then they'd run out. If anybody comes after 'em, the lady is there by the door and manages to get in the way. Makes like she's playin' with the kid or that her shopping bags spilled or somethin', but she's slowin' 'em down, ya know?"

Amos believed what the man told him and wasn't all that surprised that Millie was stooping to help Ralph in his dishonest endeavors, but to use Joey as a distraction... the very thought of it sickened him.

"Why are you helping me?" Amos asked.

The car ahead of him slowed and pulled over. Amos parked behind it and turned to his passenger to wait for an answer.

"The word is out on the streets that Ralphy's got a little kid that ain't his. That don't set well with some o' the boys, ya know? Besides, Ralphy's gettin' in our way."

The man opened the door and slipped out, quickly disappearing into a nearby alley. Two men got out of the car in front of Amos and strolled away in opposite directions. The shiny sedan moved quietly on down the street.

There was nothing for Amos to do, but wait. His heart beat wildly in anticipation. He watched as passersby stepped in and out of various businesses – a grocery store, a butcher shop, a clothing shop. All seemed normal, yet Amos knew those men had spread out and were hiding in the area. Why? What were they up to? What was he about to witness?

A curvy woman came from behind Amos' car and strolled down the street with a little boy in tow. Amos sat upright. It had been several weeks since he had seen Joey, but there weren't many little boys with big blonde curls like that. Millie had done something different with her hair and was wearing clothes he'd never seen before, but he knew it was Millie. He could tell by the way she walked. He had never noticed before how arrogant and self-assured she held herself.

Ahead of them, a portly man of Ralph's size and build was entering a store. Amos guessed Millie's aim was to stand in front of the store, thinking she would detour any pursuers. But there were dangerous men hiding nearby who wanted Ralph out of their territory.

Amos bolted out of the car as fast as his aging body would move and called to his daughter.

"Millicent Schultz! What are you doing with that boy?"

The woman slowed her pace for a moment, but didn't turn around. He raced forward and apprehended her by grabbing onto her arm. She turned on him.

"What are *you* doing here?" she hissed.

The look on her face was one of utter astonishment – and guilt. She was caught red-handed and by her father, of all people!

"Father, I have to go. I have to meet Ralph. Can we talk about this later?"

"No! Come with me now!"

"I can't!"

"Forget Ralph and come on!"

She pulled Joey and started at a brisk walk in the direction of the store.

"You go right ahead and meet Ralph, Millie. But you are not taking that boy with you."

Amos grabbed her by the wrist and wrenched her hand until she released her grip on Joey. The child whimpered in fright when Millie screamed, "Let go of me!"

Amos picked Joey up, clutched him in his arms, and said, "Good-bye, Millie."

He strode away.

Turning his back on his daughter was the hardest thing Amos had ever done. She was walking into danger and he knew it, but she had made her choice. Joey was innocent. He was the one who had to be protected. It was Joey he had come for.

Shouts behind him beckoned Amos to spin around. He had just reached his car and opened the door when gunfire exploded down the street. Ralph took off running in the direction in which he had come. He crouched behind a car and returned fire toward a figure across the street. Amos plopped Joey on the seat and slammed the passenger door shut.

"Millie, come on!" he cried.

She stopped where she was, turned toward him, and then turned back toward her husband just in time to see a man sneaking close behind Ralph – a man with a gun.

Millie screamed. Shots were being fired and Millie started running – toward Ralph. *Fool!* Amos didn't stay to watch. He hurried around the car, dove into the driver's seat, started the engine, and pushed the gas pedal. The tires squealed as he spun the car around and sped away.

Joey whimpered again. Gunshots cracked behind them.

"It's okay, Joey. Grandpa's got you. You remember Grandpa, don't you?"

"Yes," the boy said with a sob.

"You're not going to stay with Aunt Millie and Uncle Ralph any more. I'm going to take you to your mother and father. You'll like that, won't you?"

"Yes," Joey said as his countenance brightened and he offered a smile.

"And you'll see Irma and Shirley and Phillip and Harvey and Lillian. And your new little baby sister Dorothy."

"My mama got a new baby and I got to hold her. I'm not a baby anymore."

"That's right, Joey. You're not a baby anymore. You're getting to be a big boy."

Epilogue

J oey! It's good to see you again! And look at those boys of yours. Are they ever growing!"

I hadn't seen Lloyd for a number of years – probably not since Grandpa's funeral. I thought it funny that he would even recognize me, but he did. And he called me Joey. I thought I had shed that nickname decades ago.

"Have you seen your pa yet?" Lloyd asked.

"No," I answered. "We just got here."

"He was over there by the old Twin City, last I saw him. You know, he worked on some of the small engines, getting them ready for the show."

"I'm sure he did a good job."

"Oh, they sound just great! I love listening to all these old engines."

"I'm anxious to see them. We'll stop by and chat later."

The boys and I strode away from Lloyd and the steam tractor on which he was leaning. He seemed as spry as ever and talked as freely as he always did, but his voice was more gravelly than I remembered. I knew he would have liked to visit more, but if I was going to see everything at the Hungry Hollow show, I didn't want to be delayed.

Twenty-two years have gone by since I moved from my parents' farm. I now work as an engineer. My wife and I are raising three sons. They weren't too enthused about spending a fine summer Saturday looking at old stuff instead of playing baseball, but a trip from St. Paul to Grandpa's farm is always a treat for them. They agreed to come and see the gathering of Grandpa's neighbors who were displaying their old gas and steam engines and tractors.

The group has an official name now – the Hungry Hollow Steam & Gas Engine Club – and is a formal organization, but these people have been showing their old engines for a few years. On this day, they set their carefully restored machinery and expertly crafted scale models in motion. What a wonderful sight!

We found Dad right where Lloyd said he would be. He was thrilled to see us and couldn't wait to show us around. Although he is stooped and limping, he walked around most of the day.

"We had a Waterloo Boy like this," my father told his grandsons. "And there's the old Stickney we once used."

While I relished my visit to the Prock Farm, Dad delighted in sharing his knowledge of operating the old farm machinery. He explained to the boys how we split wood, pumped water, washed clothes, sawed lumber. I was pleased that I recognized small engine names like Monitor, Fairbanks and Morse, Economy, and Bessemer. I also knew what many of them were used for.

When I think back, I know I took a lot for granted when I was growing up. Being the youngest of the boys, it was not required of me to learn the mechanics of the devices used in the days before and during the Great Depression. My greatest responsibilities came after my brothers went off to war. By then Dad had acquired a number of newer, more modern pieces of equipment. In my deepest memories, I recall the smells of smoke, kerosene, and gasoline; the sounds of chugging, whirring motors; and the shrill whistle of steam engines. There were thump-thumps, the whirring and popping of engines and nose-tingling odors of smoke, burning fuels and grease – just like I was now hearing and seeing and smelling at the show.

The Depression was not hard for me. Never did I worry about whether we would have enough to eat or if we would have the means to pay for our farm. I was coddled and fed, and that was all a child in knickers needed. By the time I was old enough to become aware of the need for frugality, hard work and diligence to survive economic hardship, my family was more financially fit. But war was looming. New threats and fears were descending upon the nation. My older brothers went off to fight, my sisters did their part to help the war effort and I farmed with my father.

I did not continue with the farming life as most of my siblings did. I relished school and was the first in my family to seek higher education. I studied engineering and started a business.

Sales opportunities occasionally took me to Chicago. I visited Aunt Millie there a few times. She was a bitter soul but there was no one to blame for that except herself. My mother and father found it in their hearts to forgive her for taking me away. They extended invitations for her to come for a visit, but Aunt Millie repeatedly declined. Grandpa kept the old farmhouse for a few years in hope that she would move back to northern Wisconsin to live near her family, but she refused. I guess she reaped that which she sowed. Being envious of my mother and selfish in her desires, Millie lived in the clutches of resentment from which she was never freed. Gestures of love and kindness from our family were met with contempt. Messages of hope and encouragement went unheeded. I pray that, in the end, she made things right with the Lord… and that someone was with her.

I don't recall much of that brief stay in Chicago from which Grandpa rescued me, but there have been times when the sound of gunshots entered into my dreams. I did not see Uncle Ralph fall, but I do remember distant cries echoing in the street. Sometimes I envision the strange look on the face of Aunt Millie as Grandpa carried me away. I don't know whether that look was one of fear or anger or hatred. I never thought of asking Grandpa about it until after he had passed on.

I remember some of the long journey north. I sat on Lloyd's lap while he sang and told stories and made funny faces to entertain me. Grandpa sang, too, and we all laughed a lot.

There was great celebration when we came through the door of our big old farmhouse. My mother cried with joy and hugged me so tight I could scarcely breathe. All my brothers and sisters were there, laughing and talking, and I got to hold my little baby sister. Some of the neighbors were there. The house was crowded and loud, and the clamor of rejoicing was delightful compared to the din of the city. There was an abundance of food and I got to eat whatever I asked for. There were also welcome odors of cattle and trees and earth wafting through the open windows… and I remember the smell of rain.

Yes, to everyone's delight, it was raining.

The End

About the Author

S haron Balts and her husband Doug are Wisconsin farmers. They are frequent travelers whose vacations often include a farm show or tractor club convention. They are members of the Hungry Hollow Steam and Gas Engine Club where Doug is an exhibitor.

Unrefined is Sharon's fourth novel. It is the first historical tale set in the Great Depression era. Sharon envisions many more stories from the industrial decades that birthed the wonderful inventions we now enjoy in farm show venues.

Connect with Sharon:
www.SharonBalts.com

Hopefully you enjoyed book 1 of a collector series of novels that showcases some of America's favorite tractors, machinery, and inventions. We invite you to come along as we explore our country's rural communities, each with their unique heritage, history, and landscapes, brought to life through stories that will entertain with action, drama, adventure, and romance.

Sharon envisions many more stories from the industrial decades that birthed the wonderful inventions we now enjoy in farm show venues. Each story will be unique and can stand alone, but a number of the characters will be used in more than one story.

Farm show groups, farm museums, or tractor clubs can join the fun *and earn money*. Many stories that Sharon is working on do not have a particular line of equipment or farm show community plugged into the tale. If your group is chosen to be featured in one of these stories, your club will receive some of the proceeds for every book sold at your event or through your club contacts.

Contact Sharon Balts if you are interested in having your club featured in one of her stories. Please give her the following information:

- Club name
- Location
- Date and circumstances of founding
- Featured equipment in upcoming shows (if applicable)
- Favorite time period or special decade that might be of particular interest and why
- Major industries and agricultural commodities from that time period
- Contact name(s) and information

Write Sharon at PO Box 121, Dallas, WI 54733, email her at slbalts@chibardun.net or fill out the contact information on her website at www.SharonBalts.com.

CPSIA information can be obtained at www.ICGtesting.com
Printed in the USA
LVOW11s1552260416

485404LV00001B/170/P

9 781622 451678